Grandpa Noel's Stories

by Gary Noel

Grandpa Noel's Stories

by Gary Noel

Orange Hat Publishing
www.orangehatpublishing.com - Waukesha, WI

Published by Orange Hat Publishing 2015

ISBN 978-1-937165-86-4

Cover illustration and chapter heading
illustrations by Emily Lau

Printed in the United States of America

www.orangehatpublishing.com

Contents

Introduction

Christmas has always been a time of celebration at our house. Planning starts well before Thanksgiving. Many hours are spent preparing, cooking and baking holiday feasts, sweets and treats. Seasonal decorations transform the house into a special place.

When our oldest granddaughter, Meghan, was five, my wife, Gail, invited her to help make Christmas cookies and become part of the cooking and baking tradition. It felt like a rite of passage.

I, too, wanted to do something unique for Meghan that Christmas to celebrate her transition to a new role in the family. Whatever it was going to be, it had to be in the spirit of the season. It had to be personal and meaningful; something I did or made for her, not something I bought.

After a few false starts, I decided to write her a story, a fictional story in which she was the main character. I used the incident of her helping with Christmas cookies as the focal point and embellished the rest.

When I finished, Gail thought it would be a cute idea to read the story to Meghan on Christmas Eve with the rest of the family present. The event worked out so well, I rashly promised to write a story for each of our grandchildren in the year in which they turned five and then read it at Christmas. At the time we had six grandchildren.

Twenty-three grandchildren and twenty-one stories later (one year I combined four grandkids into two stories), Grandpa's stories are woven into the fabric of our holiday festivities. Despite the growth in our family, both in numbers and in physical size, we still crowd into our family room on Christmas Eve for the reading of the latest story. The reading normally occurs just before the younger grandchildren change into their pajamas and return to the family room to receive their Christmas book gift from Grandma and Grandpa, another tradition that has grown over the years.

After they are read, the stories are kept in a special book with a wood cover crafted by our son-in-law. The book sits in a prominent place in our living room. Often, during visits by our grandkids, it is taken from its resting place and read and reread by one or more of the kids.

Now I have completed the task, at least for the next five years, I would like to share these stories with a wider audience. Each story is a separate, stand-alone tale featuring a different child. The main character(s) and family members are real, but the story is pure fabrication. Some stories are magical, others dreamlike and a few a bit scary. The focus of all is the wonder of childhood.

To Gail, whose love and support have made all this possible.

Meghan's Story

Meghan woke up with a start. The sun was shining through the frosty window in her bedroom. She heard her younger brothers, Alex and Sean, playing downstairs. Today was a special day. Today she was going to Grandma's house to make Christmas cookies. She jumped out of bed, washed her face, brushed her teeth and went back to her bedroom to get dressed. She remembered Grandma told her to wear old clothes because she would be working with flour, chocolate and other messy stuff. As soon as she was dressed, she rushed downstairs. Sean sat in his highchair waiting for breakfast. Alex played with his Nerf football in the family room.

"Good morning, sleepy head," Mom said. "I thought you were going to sleep all morning. Did you forget that you are going to Grandma's to bake Christmas cookies today?"

"No! I can hardly wait! I can't believe Grandma said I'm big enough to help make Christmas cookies. Mom, what kinda cookies do you think we'll make?"

"I don't know. You'll have to wait until you get to Grandma's house to find out."

Meghan hurried through breakfast. After they finished, Alex asked her to play football, but Meghan wasn't listening. When Alex threw her the football that bounced off a chair, he got her attention. "Alex, I don't have time to play now. I have to get ready to go to Grandma's house to make cookies."

"I want to go to Grandma's to make cookies, too!" shouted Alex.

"You're not old enough," said Meghan. "Grandma said you have to be at least five before you can help make Christmas cookies."

Mom interrupted before the conversation could get any louder.

"Alex, get your coat and shoes. We're going to the library after we drop off Meghan."

Normally Meghan would be upset about not going to the library. It was one of her favorite places. Today was different. She quickly grabbed her coat and shoes. She even got Sean's snowsuit and gave it to Mom. She wanted to get going.

When they arrived, Meghan jumped out of the van. She rushed in the side door and called to Grandma, "Grandma, I'm here!"

At the same time she smelled the pleasant aroma of something baking. Her heart sank. She almost started to cry. She thought, *Grandma made the cookies without me.*

Grandma came to the door, waved to Meghan's mom and the boys, and gave Meghan a big hug. "You're just in time. Take off your coat. I'm just finishing making coffeecakes, and now we can start on the cookies."

Meghan smiled with relief and returned the hug.

Mom called from the van, "Dad will pick you up on his way home from work. Have fun!"

All afternoon Meghan worked with Grandma. She helped roll dough, cut out different shapes with cookie cutters, shook sprinkles on some cookies and spread jelly on others. She learned not to touch the hot cookie trays until they cooled down. She sampled any cookie she wanted.

When the other cookies were finished, Grandma told Meghan, "I've a special treat for you. We're going to make and decorate gingerbread cookies."

Grandma made the dough and Meghan cut out the shapes. She cut out daddies, mommies, boys and girls and placed them on the cookie trays.

After they baked, Grandma gave Meghan some frosting in a decorating tube and showed her how to make faces and clothes on the cookies. Meghan started with a girl. First she made eyes and eyelashes, then a tiny nose and a big smile for the mouth. She even made some curls for hair. Then Meghan added an outfit. After she was finished with that cookie, she started to decorate another one.

Concentrating on decorating the gingerbread cookies, she didn't hear her dad come in the house. When Meghan finally saw him, she gave him a big smile.

"Look at all the cookies we made. We worked really hard."

Pointing to the gingerbread cookies, she said, "These are my favorites. Grandma let me decorate them."

"I can see that," said her dad with a smile. "It looks like you and Grandma had a busy day. Mom will be excited to hear all about it."

Meghan finished her last cookie decoration and put the stool away. While she was getting her coat, Grandma made a plate of cookies to take home. When Meghan returned, Grandma said, "Pick out three gingerbread cookies. One each for Alex, Sean and you to have for dessert tonight."

Meghan picked one girl and two boys. Grandma put them in a snack bag. "Be careful so they don't break before you get home."

Meghan thanked her grandma and gave her a big hug. "I really liked making cookies with you," she said.

Grandma smiled, kissed her on the cheek and said, "Thank you for being such a big helper. We sure made a lot of cookies today."

After her dad gave Grandma a hug, they both headed out the door.

Meghan couldn't wait to tell Mom. Before taking off her coat, Meghan started jabbering about the events of the day. "Hold on," said Mom. "You can tell us all about your adventure during supper. We'll be ready in about ten minutes."

During the meal Meghan dominated the conversation. She talked about how she and Grandma worked together. She became animated when she described decorating the gingerbread cookies. Before the meal was over, Meghan hopped off her chair and ran to get the cookies Grandma had given her. She gave Alex and Sean the boy cookies, but decided to save hers.

For the rest of the evening Meghan recounted in detail the events of her day. When bedtime arrived, the rest of the family was grateful. After saying prayers and kissing her parents good night, Meghan placed her gingerbread girl on her dresser. She was still thinking about her fun day when she drifted off to sleep.

A large gingerbread cookie shook Meghan awake. This cookie looked like one that she had decorated, only a lot bigger.

"What are you doing here? What do you want?" Meghan asked. The cookie didn't say anything but beckoned Meghan to follow her. In a trance Meghan got out of bed and started to follow the cookie.

"Where are we going?" she asked anxiously.

The cookie didn't answer but rushed down a path that had the most beautiful decorations Meghan had ever seen. There were fir trees, twinkle lights, wreaths, garland and ornaments everywhere. Candies, cookies and cakes lined the road. The cookie stopped in front of a small cottage trimmed with candy and frosting. She motioned Meghan to enter. Meghan initially refused, but peeked in the window. She saw a family of gingerbread cookies. They all beckoned her.

Curiosity overcame Meghan and she eased through the door. It was very quiet in the house. The cookies motioned her to sit at the table. The table was a large flat cake with cupcakes for stools.

As soon as Meghan sat at the table, the cookies began waving their arms and shrugging their shoulders. The cookie that appeared to Meghan in her bedroom lifted Meghan's hand to her mouth. Meghan knew they were trying to tell her something, but she didn't understand their antics.

Suddenly Meghan jumped up, ran outside and walked around the cottage. Then she started up the road. She had gone a short distance when she reached down and picked up a straw lining the path. She ran back to the cottage and grabbed a handful of frosting from the trim in the back of the dwelling. She began rolling the frosting between her hands. When it was thin and soft, Meghan

4

stuffed the frosting into the straw. When the straw was full, she folded over one end and began squeezing the straw from that end.

The frosting started oozing out the open end. Meghan hurried back into the cottage. She motioned to her cookie friend to climb on the table and lie down. Meghan leaned over the cookie with the straw. All the others gathered around the table to see what Meghan was doing. They watched her draw an ear on each side of the head and a tiny tongue on the mouth. All of a sudden the gingerbread cookie jumped off the table and began making a high-pitched, squeaky sound.

Meghan's friend grabbed the mommy cookie and pulled her to the table. Meghan drew ears and a tiny tongue on the second cookie. When she was finished with that cookie, another one climbed on the table. After several of them were decorated with ears and a tongue, Meghan had to go outside to find another straw and more frosting.

All the cookies in the village began lining up for Meghan's special decoration. The noise inside the cottage increased. The high-pitched, shrill sounds were so loud that Meghan covered her ears and shut her eyes.

When she opened them, Meghan found herself back in her bedroom. She got out of bed and walked to her dresser. She looked at the gingerbread cookie and saw it had two small ears and a tiny tongue. As Meghan stared, she thought she saw the cookie wink at her.

Frances's Story

It was a beautiful, warm fall afternoon, not a cloud in the sky. Frances and Dorielle were playing in the park. Mom was sitting with Thad on a bench near the walk. All of them had just finished a picnic lunch, and the girls were playing for awhile before Dorielle and Thad had to take naps.

Dorielle ran ahead to the sandbox. Frances lagged behind and called out, "I'm going to climb on the monkey bars."

Out of the corner of her eye Frances saw a colorful object fly into one of the trees lining the parkway. She quickly turned to follow.

As she searched the trees, Frances spotted a beautiful bird sitting on one of the branches. It had a red head and bright blue and green feathers over the rest of its body. Frances remembered seeing a Baltimore oriole at Grandma's house last summer, but this bird was even more colorful. It was like a picture in a book.

She called quietly to Dorielle, but Dorielle had reached the sandbox and wasn't paying any attention. Frances didn't want to shout or make any quick movements because she didn't want the bird to fly away. Frances decided to get a closer look. *I think I can climb the tree without disturbing the bird.*

She walked quietly to the tree and began to climb. The tree had a low branch so she was able to pull herself up easily. As she slowly climbed higher, Frances kept looking at the bird to see if the bird would fly away. The bird didn't move. Frances didn't notice that the bird was watching her climb the tree. When Frances was within three feet of the bird, the bird let out a single screech that almost made Frances lose her grip. She recovered and quickly looked at the bird. She thought she heard him say, "I scared you, didn't I?"

Everyone knows that birds don't know how to talk, so Frances just stared at the bird. "Well, aren't you even going to say hello?" chirped the bird.

Frances remembered Grandpa Louie telling her about a talking parrot. "Are you a parrot?" Frances asked nervously.

"A parrot," the bird repeated. "Do I look like a parrot?"

"I don't know," replied Frances. "I'm not sure what a parrot looks like." She tried to remember if she had seen any parrots at the zoo, but she couldn't recall. "If you're not a parrot, what kind of bird are you?"

"Does it matter what kind of bird I am?" asked the bird. "Right now we have major problems and I don't have a lot of time to waste on idle chatter."

Frances wasn't sure what she should do next. She climbed up the tree to see if the bird was hurt, but she didn't expect to be sitting on a tree limb holding a conversation. *Maybe I should try to find out what the problems are so I can talk to Dad tonight. He'll know what to do.*

"If you won't tell me what kind of bird you are, will you tell me what your problems are?" responded Frances. "Maybe I can help."

"How is one little girl going to help?" said the bird. "I have to fly all over and try to find youngsters who have imagination and wonderment. With television and video games, young people don't read anymore. Consequently, no one has any creativity. Everyone tries to copy everyone else. No one has enough originality to be an individual. Look at kids' clothes, they're all the same. Television, movies, music all garbage. There isn't one thimbleful of creativity in any of it."

Frances was quiet for a moment. Then she commented, "I'm not in school yet, so I really can't help you with that problem. My cousin, Meghan, is in kindergarten, though. Maybe she could help you. My Mom and Dad say Dorielle and I have good imaginations. Sometimes they say we use our imagination too much. We play pretend a lot. It's fun pretending to be somebody else."

"Have you ever pretended that you are birds or kites trying to fly in the wind or soar in the clouds?" asked the bird.

"I never tried to be a kite," answered Frances, "but we do like to fly them. My dad takes us to the park and we see how high we can fly our kite. One time we almost ran out of string, it was so high."

"Did you ever wonder how the kite felt flying near the clouds?" the bird asked. "Maybe it was afraid of heights and didn't like being so high. Maybe it got tired after a few minutes and wanted to rest."

"That's silly," Frances replied. "Whoever talks to kites? Kites don't know how to talk. Besides, kites are supposed to fly high."

"That's exactly what I mean," answered the bird. "No imagination. Instead of wondering how a kite might feel flying in the wind, you don't even give it a thought. If the kite could talk, what would it say about flying? How do you think it likes being on the end of a string? Maybe it would like to fly solo through a cloud without someone on the ground tugging at its tail. Have you ever wondered what it's like inside the clouds? That's what real wonderment is, trying to capture the mystery of things."

"I really don't understand what you're saying," Frances commented. "First you're worried about kids not having any imagination, and now you're spouting off about talking kites. I came up here to see if you were hurt, but this is so silly."

"That's my point, exactly," said the bird. "There are so many things we don't understand, but instead of stretching our imagination and trying to learn, kids today don't seem to care. All they're interested in is television and video games. They want to be entertained constantly. They don't read books for fun anymore and they aren't interested in what's going on around them. They don't use their mind for anything except storing nonsense."

"Dorielle and I can't read yet, but my mom and dad read us books, especially at bedtime," Frances remarked. "Even Thad is starting to listen to books. We really like books."

"That's great," said the bird. "Keep asking your parents to read to you. Then learn how to read yourself. Once you know how to read, try to read different kinds of books. Challenge yourself to continue growing and learning. It will keep your curiosity and imagination alive and well. If there are more children like you, maybe there's hope for this generation after all," muttered the bird.

"FRANCES! FRANCES!"

The bird sprang out of the tree and was out of sight before Frances could say another word. She tried to see where the bird went, but it was gone, disappeared into the woods. Frances quickly scrambled down the tree and ran to her mother.

"Frances, we were looking for you. Where did you go? Dorielle wanted you to play with her in the sandbox."

"Mommy, you're not going to believe this," said Frances. "I was up in that tree talking to a magic bird. It was beautiful, with blue and green feathers and it could talk."

"You were up in a tree, talking to a magic bird, were you? And what did this magic bird have to say?" asked Mommy.

"The bird said kids today don't have an imagination, and that's a problem," responded Frances excitedly. "It also said we should continue to ask you and Dad to read to us, and then I should learn how to read by myself. If I continue to read, my imagination will remain active."

"Frances, I don't think we have to worry about your imagination remaining active," commented Mommy with a smile. "Come on now, it's time to go home. Dorielle and Thad need to take their naps. You'll have to tell Dad all about the magic bird at dinner tonight."

As she walked towards the van, Frances glanced back to see if she could see where the bird landed. All she saw were leaves fluttering in the breeze.

Alex's Story

Library night was a special night at the Noel household. Dinner was served early, so there was plenty of time to spend at the library. After finishing the meal, the older kids hurried to get ready. Meghan usually collected all the books that needed to be returned to the library. Alex and Sean got themselves ready.

No matter how often they visited the library, it was always an adventure looking through the stacks of books. Now that Alex was reading well, his dad let him pick out his own books.

The wind was howling, and a few snowflakes began to fall as they reached the library. "I guess we'll have some snow on the ground by morning," Dad said as he held the door open for the kids to enter the library. "Maybe you should pick out an extra book in case we get snowed in."

Alex wasn't concerned about the weather. He wanted to get in the library to begin exploring for new books. When they reached the children's section, Dad told Meg and Alex, "You can look by yourselves for a little while. I'll be with Sean."

Alex remembered he had seen some baseball stories the last time he was at the library, and he wanted to find them. He headed for the section he thought contained sports books. While Alex was browsing, he spotted a book titled *Alexander's Valuable Lesson*. He slid the book from the shelf and began to page through it. He decided to take a closer look before he continued his search. He found an empty chair, sat down and began to read.

****

Alexander Anderson was eight years old, and he was miserable. He was a northern transplant living in Charleston, South Carolina. He and his family had recently relocated from Chicago after his dad was promoted to Southern Regional Sales Manager.

Alexander was upset about the change. His whole world had turned upside down. He knew this new position was important to his father, but he didn't understand why they had to move. Despite living in a new home in a very nice area, he was miserable. Alexander missed his friends and his old neighborhood.

Alexander started at the new school midway through the school year. He felt alone.

His mother knew he was struggling with the change. When she dropped him off at school each morning, she always parted with a positive comment. "Have a great day!" "Have fun today!" "Enjoy your classes!"

Every afternoon when she picked him up, his mother asked him two questions. "How was your day? Did you make any new friends?"

Every day Alexander had to tell her, "My day was okay, but I didn't make any new friends."

He acted as if he didn't care, but it hurt that none of the other kids seemed to like him.

After more than a week of similar responses, his mother became more direct. "Alexander, you have to make more of an effort to make a friend. You have to initiate a conversation or volunteer for a project. Don't wait for someone else to take the first step. You have to do it."

Trying to take her advice, Alexander came up with a plan to make friends. He would be first in everything the class did. If they were reading a story, he would be the first one to read. If they were doing work, he had to finish first. If his teacher asked a question, he would be first to raise his hand. It didn't matter what they were doing, he was going to be first. He wanted to show everyone in the class he was the best so they would have to like him.

The next afternoon Mrs. Jefferson made a special announcement to the class. "My husband is coaching a community soccer team for eight- and nine-year-old boys. Tryouts for the team will be next week starting on Tuesday from six to seven thirty p.m. at the soccer field behind the community center. I'm passing out information sheets on the team. Anyone interested in trying out must have the permission slip signed by a parent. Bring the signed slip with you to the first day of tryouts."

Alexander read the announcement and knew this tryout fit into his plan. He had played soccer in Chicago. Now he would show his new classmates how good he was.

When his mom picked him up after school and asked him about his day, Alexander quickly showed her the soccer team announcement.

"This could be fun for you. We'll talk about it with Dad when he gets home from work."

"Mom, I really want make this soccer team. This is my chance to finally get some friends."

"I didn't say you couldn't. I said we'll talk about it with your dad."

As soon as his father was in the house, Alexander almost knocked him over trying to hand him the announcement.

"Dad, I really want play on this team!"

After reading the information and briefly discussing it with his wife, both agreed that the soccer team might be good for Alexander.

"You can try out, but don't be disappointed if you don't make the team. These kids may have been playing together for a while. Remember, you're new to this area."

"You don't have to remind me."

At the designated time of the first practice, eighteen boys were eager to show their soccer skills. After the coach conducted drills for the entire practice, he called the group together.

"I want to thank y'all for coming out tonight. We had a good workout. I saw a lot of positive things from many of you. We have eighteen players here tonight. Unfortunately, it's too many for one team. A soccer team for this age group normally has no more than fifteen on the team. We'll have two more practices and then I'll decide how we're going to deal with the numbers. The next practice will be Thursday at six p.m.."

Alexander wasn't concerned about what the coach said about the number of players because he had performed well. He knew he was one of the better players.

The next day at school Timmy Dempsey came up to Alexander at recess.

"I watched you at the soccer tryout last night. You're good. I want to make this team but I'm terrible. Will you help me get better?"

Alexander didn't know Timmy very well, but he said, "Sure, I'll try to help. Let's get a soccer ball from the gym and get started."

For the next two days at recess Alexander practiced with Timmy. They worked on dribbling, passing and controlling the ball. Since they didn't have a goal for shooting, they kicked the ball between two trees to score goals. After two days, Timmy started kicking with more confidence.

At the second practice Alexander tried to watch how Timmy was performing, but he also had to pay attention to what he himself was doing. When it was over, Alexander walked with Timmy to the parking lot. Timmy had his head down.

"I'm not good enough to make this team. I'm wasting my time."

Alexander tried to console him. "You did fine. Don't worry. We have one more tryout before the coach picks the team. We'll keep working at school. You're getting better. You really are!"

****

"Alex, are you ready? The snow's coming down harder, so we'd better get going."

Alex jumped off the chair and headed to the book stacks. He randomly grabbed four other books along with the book he had been reading.

When they arrived home, Mom was waiting with hot chocolate and graham crackers. While the kids drank their hot chocolate, Mom looked at the books they brought from the library.

"Alex, I didn't know that you were interested in stamp collecting. Did you really want a book on how to start a stamp collection?"

Alex tried to explain. "I was reading a book and Dad wanted to get going. I didn't have much time so I just grabbed a few books from the shelf."

At bedtime Alex was eager to continue reading his book. He put on his pajamas, kissed his parents goodnight and jumped into bed with his library book. He already had his flashlight on when

13

Sean came into the bedroom. Sean wanted to talk.

"Sean, I'm trying to read. Go to sleep."

Sean got the message and quieted down. Alex returned to his book.

****

The next day at recess Alexander grabbed a soccer ball and looked for Timmy. He saw him with a small group of classmates. Alexander walked over to the cluster of kids and asked Timmy, "Are you ready?"

"I don't think I am going to play soccer today."

"Why not? We only have a few days and one more practice until the coach makes the final selection. You said you wanted to make the soccer team."

One of the group chimed in. "Alexander's right. If you want to make the team, you have to keep practicing."

"Okay," Timmy agreed reluctantly.

Several classmates joined them in a soccer game. Timmy was on Alexander's team. Instead of trying to be the best, Alexander worked with Timmy. He passed him the ball whenever he could. He paid more attention to Timmy than he did to the game. When the bell rang, the group agreed to continue the game tomorrow. For the first time since he started at the new school, Alexander returned to the classroom happy.

That afternoon his mom asked him the standard questions. "How was your day? Did you make any new friends?"

Alexander broke into a big smile. "I've been practicing soccer with Timmy at recess. Now more kids want to help. We had a soccer game today and everyone wants to play again tomorrow. It's funny. I wanted to get people to like me by being first at everything, but nobody paid any attention to me. Now that I'm trying to help Timmy, suddenly I have friends."

"Alexander, maybe you just learned a valuable lesson. When you think only about yourself, no one else cares. When you try to help someone else, then the group welcomes you."

****

Alex turned the page, excited to find out if Timmy made the soccer team. The End stared back at him. He slammed the book closed. *How could the book end that way?* He rolled over and punched his pillow.

The next morning at breakfast Alex told his mom about his frustration with the ending of the book.

"Why did the book end that way? I don't know if Timmy made the soccer team or if Alexander got any new friends!"

"Alex, take some time and think about why the author ended the story the way he did. Also, you could pretend you are the author and write a different ending to the story."

Winter in Minnesota is good for both thinking and writing.

Christopher's Story

Christopher was in bed trying to go to sleep. He had read for awhile, but he still wasn't tired. Suddenly he heard a shrill noise coming from his closet. Christopher knew his mom didn't like him getting out of bed at night, but the sound persisted. It sounded like a high-pitched voice calling his name. He lifted his head and stared at his brother's bed. He thought Andrew might disguising his voice and calling out. Andrew was sound asleep.

Christopher grabbed his flashlight off the nightstand and crept quietly toward the closet. He didn't want to disturb Andrew and he certainly didn't want his mom hear him get out of bed. He opened the door very slowly and shined the light into the closet. His heart began to pound.

At first he didn't see anything. He felt relieved. He continued to shine the light around the closet. When he was about to close the door, he saw something move in the far corner. He froze. He couldn't decide if he should close the door quickly and jump back in bed or find out what was in his closet. Curiosity won.

Pointing the light at the spot where he saw movement, a silhouette of a little person dressed in a robe and hood appeared on the back wall. As he crouched forward to get a better look, Christopher thought it looked like a character from Star Wars. The little person had large eyes and curly hair. He began waving to Christopher, encouraging him to come closer.

Christopher wasn't sure he wanted to stay in the closet, but decided he had to find out who this person was. After all, the character was about the size of his Buzz Lightyear toy, so how dangerous could he be? He saw the little person reach his hand into a little pouch tied around his waist and throw some glittering powder into the air. While Christopher watched the sparkling flakes dance in the flashlight beam, he suddenly felt very sluggish. He couldn't move or utter a sound.

The stranger quickly grabbed one of Christopher's arms and tied a rope around his wrist. Christopher tried to resist but he could barely move. The stranger pulled the arm behind Christopher's back and then repeated the procedure with the other arm. Christopher slumped to the floor.

When he woke up, Christopher was flat on his back, tied securely on a bed of sticks. This platform was carried by eight other little people, all wearing brown robes like the stranger in Christopher's closet. He looked around and didn't recognize anything. He tried to free himself but he could only move his head. He tried to scream but only faint sounds came out of his mouth. Christopher felt so alone and helpless that tears began to well up in his eyes. He started to cry.

The tears got the attention of his carriers. They stopped moving and put him down. The little man he had seen in the closet approached him while he was lying on the ground.

He asked softly, "Why are you crying, Christopher?"

Christopher looked at him through watery eyes. He was surprised the individual knew his name. Christopher whispered in a hoarse, tearful voice, "You sneaked into my bedroom, sprinkled something on me, and tied me up. Now your group is taking me somewhere. Why am I crying? I'm crying because I don't know what's happening to me and I'm afraid."

"Christopher," responded the little person, "we won't hurt you. We need your help. The only way we could get your help was to bring you to our land. I had to use the magic dust to quiet you so we could bring you here. The spell isn't permanent. I can't tell you any more right now. You will learn our plan soon. In the meantime, if I untie you will you promise not to run away?"

"Where would I run?" queried Christopher. "I don't know where I am, how I got here, or how to get away. Right now I can't do anything. Why me?"

"That will be answered in due time," answered the little man.

As he spoke, he began to untie Christopher from the platform. When he stood up, a few members of the group quickly hid the platform in some underbrush. After stretching for a minute Christopher began to look closely at his surroundings. He had to figure out a way back home.

Even though the little man said the magic dust wasn't permanent, Christopher was concerned. As he rubbed his wrists, he noticed he was still wearing his pajamas. Almost as if his captor was reading his mind, he handed Christopher a brown robe similar to the ones that everyone else was wearing. When Christopher slipped the robe over his head, he was amazed that it fit. After a few minutes, the group began walking toward a large mountain.

Everyone moved in silence. Christopher was able to keep pace with the others. He continued looking around, trying to find something he recognized. After what seemed forever, Christopher had to talk to someone. He asked the person next to him, "Where are we and where are we going?"

The person looked at him but didn't say anything. Very quickly the little person who had been in his closet was next to him. Christopher decided he must be some kind of leader because he had been in front of the group until Christopher began asking questions.

"Christopher," the little person said, "our people don't normally talk. Although we have vocal cords, we normally use brain waves to communicate. All the time you thought we were walking in silence, there have been several conversations going on within the group. Many are wondering if you are going to be able to help us. I keep telling them you were chosen for a special reason, and when the critical time comes, we'll be able to depend on you. I know you're trying to find a way to escape. You would be better to spend your time appreciating the beauty of our land instead of trying to escape from it. Remember, we can read brain waves."

Now Christopher didn't know what to do. *If these little people really can read my mind, how can I plan an escape without them knowing? I have to continue this adventure until an opportunity for escape presents itself.*

Finally they reached the base of the mountain and began to ascend. Parts of the path were so narrow they had to walk single file. After one curve, those in the front started to enter a crevice in the mountain that was barely visible.

Inside the opening was a long and narrow cave. At the far end was another opening that was partially covered by a large rock. Three or four of the little people grabbed a large pole next to the rock and pried the rock away from the opening.

After crawling on all fours through the cave, Christopher squeezed through the opening. When his eyes adjusted to the dim light, he saw a large room carved out of the rock. He was able to stand up straight.

There were many little people in the room. The leader of his group walked quickly to the far side of the room and seemed to be communicating with another little person sitting at a large round table. Although Christopher didn't hear any sounds, they were nodding and moving their arms as if they were having a conversation. After several minutes the little person Christopher knew came back and motioned to Christopher to come with him.

Christopher reluctantly began to walk toward the table. As he did so, the person rose from his chair. Although no taller than the others, this one looked older. He had a wrinkly face and a long beard.

"Welcome to our village, Christopher," he said in a soft, low voice.

He extended his hand to Christopher. Hesitantly, Christopher shook the hand of the stranger.

"Christopher, I'm sure you're very confused about what's happening to you. I will try to explain what is going on and why we need your help. My name is Advisor."

As he was talking, he motioned Christopher to have a seat. "Our village is in a great crisis. We are a peaceful people. We have lived with our neighbors without conflict for many, many years.

"Recently our neighbor to the north chose a new leader. This new leader is aggressive and has begun making trouble for all his neighbors. He invited several elders from neighboring villages for a meeting. Now he is holding them captive. He has threatened to harm them unless each village declares him as their leader.

"The captives are heavily guarded so any rescue attempt would result in many people getting hurt. We don't want to risk the lives of our people in a confrontation, so we have devised a secret rescue plan."

"How can I help?" asked Christopher. "I'm only a boy."

"Yes, I know," said Advisor, "but you are a very intelligent boy. Also, you have a special name."

"What's my name have to do with anything?" asked Christopher.

"In our culture," said Advisor, "we do not name babies when they are born. We wait until they are old enough to earn a name. When that time comes, there is a special naming ceremony by the village. Each name has a special significance. It gives the person unique powers. For example, the person whom you met in your closet is named Wizard. He is very cunning and has magical powers. The reason we chose you to help us is your name. The name Christopher has special importance. The legendary Christopher carried people out of danger. That is what we want you to do. Carry our people back to us."

As Advisor was talking, Christopher heard someone calling his name.

"CHRISTOPHER! What are you doing in the closet?" Mom asked in amazement. "Did you sleep here all night?"

Christopher opened his eyes and saw he was back in his bedroom closet. His flashlight was next to him and his mom was standing in the doorway. He jumped up and gave her a big hug.

"I didn't know if I'd ever see you again. The little people tied me up and took me to their village. They used magic dust and could even read brain waves. They wanted me to help them get

20

back their elders. They thought I could help because of my name."

His mom looked at him in amazement. "Slow down, Christopher, everything is fine. You're in your bedroom and we're all here. That must have been some dream! Just one thing, Christopher. Please try to stay in bed tonight!"

Dorielle's Story

Dorielle Jean followed Frances off the school bus. Both of them waved to their mom, who was waiting at the corner with Thad. Mom had a habit of quickly checking their faces to see how the day had gone.

Mom saw Dorielle was beaming. As soon as she exited the bus, Dorielle started talking. "Our class is reading a story about knights, dragons and a magician. Mrs. Raft told us there's an exhibit at the museum that has gowns, armor and other stuff from that time. She's arranging a class visit to the museum to see the display. Isn't that great? It's going to be so much fun!"

Frances tried to tell her mother about something that happened at school, but Dorielle kept talking. Frances shrugged her shoulders. She would wait until DJ wound down.

Dorielle continued as they entered the house. Finally her mother put up her hand. "Stop. Wait until dinner so your father can share in all your excitement."

When her dad got home, DJ greeted him with a big hug and told him, "I have a surprise for you at supper. Mom said I couldn't say anything until then, so hurry and get ready."

Dorielle helped Frances set the table so they could start eating. In her haste to put the silverware down, she bumped a glass of milk and it spilled all over the table and floor. She rushed to get some paper towels and helped wipe up the mess. Instead of eating sooner, it was taking forever to get started.

Meanwhile, Dad wondered what the surprise might be. Sometimes his girls lived in a fantasy world, so he was never sure what their imaginations had in store for him. He figured it must be something to do with school, but he would have to wait until they started eating before finding out.

Finally, the spilled milk was cleaned up and everyone was at the table. When the blessing was over, Dorielle started talking about the field trip. She told her dad about the story they were reading in school. Mrs. Raft thought it would be nice for the students to see what a knight's armor looked like. The museum had a display of these items, so they were going to visit the museum.

After Dorielle slowed down, her dad asked her, "Do you remember the library book we read last year about the knight who had rescued a maiden from the dragon's cave?"

"I'm not sure, but could we please go to the library tonight and get it so we could read it again before the field trip? Please, please!"

Since DJ was so enthused about this trip, Dad agreed. "Reading is always a good thing. Besides, we all might learn something about medieval England."

After a quick conversation Dad and Mom decided to take the whole family to the library. Dorielle rushed through the rest of her meal and begged everyone else to hurry. Even Thad cooperated and all of them finished dinner quickly.

When they arrived at the library, they all headed to the children's section. They had decided in the van they could only spend about thirty minutes in the library, so they had to make every minute count. Frances went off by herself to pick out some books. Dad and DJ went directly to the librarian's desk to search for books about knights. Mom stayed with Thad.

After hearing their request, the librarian checked her computer listing and wrote down the titles of five books that were currently in the library. Dad and Dorielle headed to the fiction section to look for the books. They found them quickly and began to look for Frances. When they spotted her, Frances already had an armful of books and was ready to go. Mom was in the play section occupying Thad. They quickly checked out the books and were back in the van in twenty-five minutes.

After getting ready for bed, Dorielle asked her mom to read them one of the books she got from the library. Even though she was tired, DJ forced herself to stay awake and listen to the book. Finally, her mom stopped reading, kissed the girls goodnight, turned off the light and quietly closed the door.

When her mom left, Dorielle whispered to Frances, "Have you ever seen a real magician? In the book Mrs. Raft is reading, there's a magician who can cast a spell on people and turn them into trees and other things. It's kinda scary."

Frances was tired. "Can we talk about this tomorrow? I just wanna go to sleep."

After that comment, Frances rolled over and fell asleep immediately. Since DJ had no one else to question, she hugged her pillow and closed her eyes.

The next several days passed by quickly. Mrs. Raft continued to read the story and talk about the museum.

Finally the big day arrived. Dorielle woke up early and couldn't wait for the bus. She put on her favorite dress and asked her mom to fix her hair a special way.

When her mom finished combing Dorielle's hair, she said, "DJ, you've been so excited about this field trip, I can't imagine what you're going to be like for your first school dance."

When the bus door swung open, Dorielle sprang up the steps, waved to her mom and announced to the driver, "I'm going on a field trip today."

The bus driver surprised DJ. "I know. I'm going to drive your class to the museum."

When the bus arrived at school, the driver asked Dorielle to tell her teacher that the bus for the museum would be waiting in the parking lot. Dorielle ran quickly to her classroom.

"Mrs. Raft, the bus for the museum is in the parking lot."

With that information Mrs. Raft encouraged everyone to get ready. Each of the children had a designated partner for the bus trip and the museum tour. Dorielle had chosen Sandy as her partner. They were to sit together on the bus and stay with each other at the museum.

When the bus arrived at the museum, a woman was waiting for them at the door.

"I'm Mrs. Jonas and I will be your guide for the tour. We'll start in the meeting room in the building. I'll briefly talk about some of the things that you will be seeing. I know you are eager to get started, but there are a few rules you must follow. First, try to stay together in the group. Don't wander off by yourself. Second, keep the noise down. There are other people in the museum. You can talk, but don't yell or shout. Third, don't touch the displays. Some of them are very old and could be damaged if you handle them."

Mrs. Jonas knew the children were impatient to get started. After a brief talk about the exhibits, she told everyone, "Find your partner and we'll walk quietly to the medieval England room."

Mrs. Jonas led the group and Mrs. Raft stayed in the back to make sure there were no stragglers. As they turned the corner, the class slowed down when they saw a statue dressed in full armor in front of the large room. It had a lance in one hand and a sword in the other.

Mrs. Jonas stopped to explain, "This is how a knight dressed before going into battle. Our knight stands guard protecting the room."

Then the class entered the large room and saw displays of armor, banners, shields, lances, swords and gowns. There was even a knight on a horse all dressed in armor. The class started to go in several directions. Fortunately, there was no one else in the room, so the children could wander around without disturbing anyone else. Mrs. Raft and Mrs. Jonas tried to keep an eye on everyone.

Dorielle saw the display of gowns and started to walk toward them. Since she was still holding Sandy's hand, Sandy reluctantly followed. Dorielle stood before the exhibit and was in awe of all the beautiful dresses, jewelry and scarves. As she wandered around the display, she separated from Sandy, who made her way over to the knight on horseback. As she gazed at all the finery, Dorielle began to imagine the fun she and Frances could have dressing up in these gowns. She closed her eyes and tried to imagine how she would look in a long, flowing gown.

Suddenly Dorielle was in a strange room wearing one of the dresses. She didn't know where she was or how she got there. A loud knock on a door shattered the silence. She looked around the room and saw no one. The knocking continued. She crept to the door and called out timidly, "Who's there?"

She heard a muffled voice saying, "Open the door."

"I'm sorry, I'm not supposed to open a door to a stranger," Dorielle responded.

While she was still huddled behind the closed door holding her breath, another person appeared in the room. She looked at him in amazement. "How did you get in here? The door's still closed and yet you're in the room."

As Dorielle spoke to him, she observed the strange-looking person. He was short, had a rather pointed nose and long curly hair down to his shoulders. He had a scraggly beard and was dressed completely in black. His dark eyes sparkled as he smiled at her.

"I know you don't know me, but I'm trying to help you," said the strange person. "As far as how I got into the room, a bit of magic, but nothing too difficult. I'm here because I'd like to help you find some friends. I saw you standing by yourself at the museum. You looked lonely. No child should be lonely. I'll take you to meet Lady Judith. She's looking for a young maiden to be a playmate for her children. She will also introduce you to the other children. I think you'll do fine."

"There must be some mistake," responded Dorielle. "I don't know where I am or how I got here, but I sure don't want to go anywhere with you. I don't even know you. I was at the museum with my class looking at the gowns and now I'm here."

"There's no mistake," responded the little man. "I brought you here to our world."

"Why me?" responded Dorielle, almost shouting and crying at the same time. "My teacher will be looking for me. My mom and dad are expecting me home tonight. My sister, Frances, will be waiting for me on the school bus after school this afternoon."

"Don't worry about any of them," said the stranger. "I'll cast a spell over the lot of them so they won't remember you at all."

"How can you say, 'Don't worry about my family?' I want to be with my family. And I do have friends. Sandy and I were partners, but we just got separated. I want to go back. I don't want to be here!" DJ shouted at the little man.

"Don't be alarmed," said the magician. "Nothing bad will happen to you or your family. I know you'll learn to enjoy our way of living soon enough. You can dress in gowns like this every day. I just want you to be happy and have friends."

He extended his hand. Dorielle pulled away and looked around for an escape. She was standing close to the door. She grabbed the handle on the big door and began to pull.

Suddenly an alarm went off. There was a loud ringing throughout the building. Dorielle froze. As she turned back to the magician, he disappeared in a puff of smoke.

She was back at the museum. She looked around and saw everyone running toward the knight on the horse. She quickly moved to the same location and heard Ms. Jonas explain what happened.

"A group of boys were looking at the display and one of them reached over the barrier to try and touch the knight's sword. That set off the alarm. I told all of you before we started not touch any of the items on display."

Dorielle looked around the room. Everything looked the same. She wasn't sure what had just happened, but she was happy to be back in the museum. She saw Sandy begin to walk toward the display of banners.

"Wait for me," Dorielle called to Sandy. "I'm definitely staying with you for the rest of the tour."

On the bus back to school, Dorielle thought to herself, *Wait until I tell everyone at home about this field trip.*

Andrew's Story

Andrew enjoyed school. Every day had something new and different. He liked his teacher, Mrs. Wagner, and he had made friends with many of his classmates. He even liked riding the bus.

Today Andrew got off the bus and hurried into the house. He proudly announced to his mother, "I have a project for school. Mrs. Wagner said we have to make up a story to tell the class. It can be about anything we want."

He reached into his backpack, pulled out a sheet of paper and handed to his mom. His teacher had written, "The class is talking about the wonderful gift of imagination. I plan to give various assignments during the school year to allow the children to use their imagination.

"In this first project, each child is to pretend that he or she is a librarian in charge of story hour. Instead of reading a story, each child must tell a story. The story has to be something made up; it cannot be something that actually happened. The child telling the story should be involved in the story in some way. The tale can be as long or as short as the child wishes it to be. Parents can help the children prepare, but I want the children to be the main story tellers."

"This will be a fun project for you, Andrew," said Mom. "You have a good imagination and you like to tell stories. Do you have an idea about what kind of story you are going to tell?"

"No," answered Andrew. "I'll have to think about it. Mrs. Wagner said we should start with something we like and build a story around it."

At dinner that night Andrew told his brother Christopher about his school project. For the rest of the meal the family began reminiscing about funny or interesting things that happened to them that could be used as a framework for a story. They recalled the camping expedition at Grandma's last summer when a late night storm almost blew over the tent. That was a painful memory for Andrew because many of his baseball cards got wet from rain in the tent.

They chuckled about the night the fully decorated Christmas tree fell during a dinner party. They laughed about Aunt Margie's homemade Halloween piñata that wouldn't break. When the meal was over, Andrew had a lot of ideas.

That night before going to bed Andrew played with his baseball cards. Even though the baseball season was almost over, he still enjoyed looking at the different players and playing pretend baseball games. Andrew heard his mom call, "It's time for bed. Put away your cards and get ready."

When he crawled under the covers, he tried to decide about the story, but he was too tired. He drifted off to sleep.

Suddenly he was wide awake. Standing in his room was someone who looked like Tony Womack, the Arizona Diamondbacks' second baseman. Andrew recognized him from his baseball card.

"Hurry up," encouraged Tony. "We have to get going. Brenly gets upset with his players if they're not dressed and on the field at least three hours before game time. Tonight's game with the Brewers is important. That's why you have to be available."

Andrew was confused, but Tony insisted that he get ready. "Come on, let's go!"

Andrew put on his school clothes and hurried downstairs. His mother was waiting for him at the door. She gave him a kiss, wished him good luck and encouraged him to play well. She told him the whole family would be at tonight's game and they would meet him after the game.

Tony's car was in the driveway and he told Andrew to jump in the passenger's seat. "I'd rather sit in the back seat," said Andrew.

Tony shrugged and got in the driver's seat. He drove quickly out of the subdivision and headed for the freeway.

As he drove, he told Andrew, "My ankle is still too sore to play regularly. That's why the Diamondbacks have added you to the roster. The manager wanted someone on the bench fast enough to be a pinch runner if they need one in the late innings."

Andrew couldn't believe Tony Womack was talking to him like he was a teammate. As they approached Miller Park, they headed to the reserved parking area. The parking attendant recognized Tony and directed him to a parking space. Tony was out of the car and opening the trunk before Andrew could get out of his seat belt. When Andrew finally got out of the car, Tony was heading for the players' entrance.

Andrew caught up with him as they entered the stadium. Tony waved to the security guard and headed towards the visitors locker room. Andrew had to trot to keep up with Tony. He didn't want to fall behind and then have someone ask him where he thought he was going.

When they entered the visitors locker room, Tony said, "I'm going to the trainer's room for treatment on my ankle. Get ready and don't wait for me. I'll see you on the field."

Andrew panicked. He couldn't leave because he wasn't sure if he could find the way out of the stadium. Even if he found his way out, what would he do then? He did recall his mom had told him the whole family would be at the game and meet up afterwards.

Andrew stood frozen inside the entrance to the locker room. He felt very alone. There was a lot of activity, but no one paid any attention to him. Some people were playing cards while others were in small groups talking. A few guys were on training tables getting a rub down. Then he saw his name, Trafton, taped above one of the lockers. His eyes grew large and he almost shouted. In the open locker he saw a uniform on a hanger and a hat on the shelf. His last name was on the jersey. He spotted a pair of spikes and a glove on the floor of the locker. It was his glove. He couldn't contain the smile as he walked to the locker.

"Welcome to the bigs, kid," said a voice. Andrew looked up at a ballplayer who was standing in front of the locker next to the one marked Trafton. He extended his hand. Andrew shook it and quietly said, "Thanks." He kept his head down because he didn't want anyone to see how nervous he was.

"Try on your uniform to make sure it fits. If there is a problem, the equipment manager is around somewhere. He should be able to help. Some of the guys might make fun of you because of your size, but they don't mean anything by it. I can still remember the razzing I got from some of these guys when I joined the team. They called me Professor because I went to Notre Dame. You'll get used to it."

As the player moved away, Andrew saw the name Counsell on the locker next to his. *Craig Counsell!* Andrew thought. *The hero of the 2001 World Series shook my hand and welcomed me to the team. Christopher is never going to believe this!*

Andrew followed Craig Counsell's advice and quickly changed into his uniform. It fit perfectly. He wanted to look in a mirror, but he was concerned the other players might make fun of him. He was still standing in front of the locker when someone dressed in a baseball uniform came into the room and asked for their attention. Andrew thought he might be the manager or a coach because he looked much older. The guys gathered around the man.

"We have a new player for tonight's game—Andrew Trafton," the man said. "Andrew's fast so he might see some action as a pinch runner."

There were a few shouts of welcome from the group. The man concluded the quick meeting with the remark that the team bus was leaving for the airport forty-five minutes after the game so everyone should be showered, bags packed and ready to go by that time.

Andrew didn't understand what he meant about the team bus and the airport. Then someone shouted, "Everyone on the field in five minutes."

The players scattered, grabbing their gloves and hats and putting on their jerseys. They moved out of the locker room, walked down a hall and through the dugout, and headed to the field. Andrew quickly put on his baseball shoes and snatched his glove and hat from the locker. He followed the rest of the group.

As he walked onto the field, Andrew gazed at his surroundings. He was on the baseball field at Miller Park, playing with the Arizona Diamondbacks.

Andrew looked around and saw the players begin their pre-game stretching. He lined up with some of the other players and tried to follow what they were doing. After stretching for awhile, some of the players began playing catch while others were standing around the batting cage waiting for their turn to hit. A few were running in the outfield.

As Andrew stood on the outfield grass wondering what he should do next, one of the coaches called him to the dugout. "I want to go over the signs so you'll know them if you get in the game. To start, nothing matters until I go to my hat with my right hand and then directly to my chest with the same hand. That's the trigger. The next sign I give after the trigger is the actual sign. The steal sign is right hand on left arm. The take sign is right hand on right ear. The hit and run sign is left hand on right arm. The bunt sign is right hand on the hat."

The coach demonstrated each sign. He ran through them one more time and asked Andrew if he understood. Andrew's head was spinning as he tried to follow the coach's maneuvers. He nodded yes, but wasn't sure if he knew the signs.

Most of the team returned to the dugout and some of the players went back to the locker room. Andrew sat very quietly at the end of the bench. He again thought about the team bus leaving for the airport forty-five minutes after the game.

Did that mean me? Am I really a member of the Diamondbacks? How am I going to tell my family that I can't meet them after the game because I have to be on the team bus? What about school?

The sounds of "The Star-Spangled Banner" shook Andrew out of his trance. With his hat over his heart he stood next to the other players while the music played. As the final notes floated over the stands, he heard the umpire call out, "Play ball!"

Tony sat next to Andrew during the early innings. As the game went on, Tony tried to explain some of the strategy that occurs during the game. From his vantage point in the dugout, Andrew was amazed at how much bigger the players were and how much faster the pitchers threw the ball. It wasn't the same as sitting in the stands or watching on television. After the sixth inning Tony said he was going back to the locker room to do some stretching and hit off a tee. With the excitement of the game, Andrew forgot about his after-the-game problem.

In the bottom of the eighth inning, Tony came back to the dugout. Since the pitcher was due to bat second in the top of the ninth and the score was tied, Tony thought he might pinch-hit for the pitcher. When the inning started, Bob Brenly shouted to Tony, "Loosen up. You're hitting second this inning."

Andrew watched Tony go to the bat rack, pick out his bat and move to the on-deck circle. After Miller hit a fly ball to left for the first out, Tony stepped into the batter's box. He hit the second pitch right up the middle for a single. Tony ran to first but he limped noticeably. When the ball was thrown back to the pitcher, Brenly yelled, "Time. Trafton, run for Womack."

Andrew almost tripped on the top step as he jumped out of the dugout. His heart was racing as he trotted to first base. Tony gave him a high five and yelled, "Show the Milwaukee fans what you can do."

Before Andrew reached first base, the coach called him over and whispered in his ear, "I know the signs are complicated, so when I call your first name, you take off for second. Do you understand?"

Andrew nodded and went to the bag. He was standing on first base at Miller Park with more than twenty thousand fans looking at him. He knew his family was somewhere in the crowd. He told himself, "Relax, concentrate on the pitcher's move and don't worry about the crowd."

He took a short lead as the pitcher went into his stretch. The pitcher glanced over once, twice and then began his motion toward the plate. "Andrew!" the coach yelled.

As soon as he heard his name he started racing for second base.

"Andrew! Andrew! Come on, get up. We have to get ready for school."

Andrew heard Christopher's voice, opened his eyes and looked around. There was no Miller Park, no screaming fans and no Diamondback players. He was in his bedroom with Christopher standing over his bed. Andrew snapped his eyes closed to recapture the game, but it was gone.

When Andrew and Christopher came downstairs a few minutes later, Mom asked, "Andrew, what's the matter? You usually come bounding into the kitchen, but this morning you're really dragging."

Andrew looked up and said, "Christopher just ruined the best dream I ever had. But," he continued, "I know what my school story is going to be."

Sean's Story

It was an early fall evening, but the temperature was almost summer-like. Taking advantage of the warm evening, Sean, Alex and Dad were in the backyard hitting a few grounders.

"Okay, Seanny, here it comes," called Dad from one side of the yard.

Sean crouched and got ready for the ball. Dad hit the ball and it came on two bounces. He attempted to field it, but didn't get his glove in front of the ball. It bounded by him. Sean turned and chased after it. When he picked up the ball, he pounded it into his glove as if to show it where it was supposed to go.

After several more hits and a few catches, Dad decided they needed a break. All three grabbed their water bottles and headed for the deck.

"Dad," Sean asked between sips as he was relaxing in a chair, "why are you still going to school? You already went to college and you have a good job."

Dad paused before he attempted to answer the question. He wasn't sure why Sean had asked, but he wanted to make sure Sean and the rest of the kids understood how important an education is for their future.

"Sean, let me answer your question with a question. Why do we practice grounders in the backyard?"

"Because it's fun," Sean responded without any hesitation.

Although that wasn't the answer Dad had hoped to hear, he certainly couldn't disagree. "That's right, Sean. Practicing to improve yourself can be fun. Going to school is the same thing.

Learning new things is fun. Remember the first time you tried to read a book, jump rope or catch a baseball? You couldn't do it very well. Learning's like that. You grow and develop through learning. Also, it helps on the job."

As Sean sat on the deck thinking about what Dad had said, he tried to imagine what it would be like to be a grown up. Maybe he would be a baseball player or a doctor or an astronaut. He began to wonder what it would be like to fly in space.

"Doctor Noel, Doctor Noel! Please respond immediately on the security channel."

The sound resonated from the telecommunicator on his belt. Sean picked up the instrument as he walked down the corridor and quickly switched on the decoder. He had been at the NASA Astronaut Training Center for six months and this was the first time he had received a personal call. He wasn't sure how to answer the call because he was still learning the military customs and ways of doing things.

"This is Doctor Noel. I'm on the security channel. Go ahead, please."

"Sean, this is Colonel Gaylord. Proceed to the planning room in the security area immediately. There is a briefing in fifteen minutes regarding the new space station, and I want you there."

"I'm on the way, Colonel. I should arrive in ten minutes."

Sean signed off and immediately headed for the security area. He wasn't sure why he was being included in the briefing, but he could tell from Colonel Gaylord's voice that this was not going to be a routine meeting.

Sean had not been in that area of the complex since his initial orientation to the Space Center. He recalled how proud he felt the first time he had arrived at the NASA complex in Houston. Out of the thousands who had applied, he was the only civilian and only medical doctor chosen for a new astronaut training class. All the other members were military.

He became interested in the space program after he had completed two years of specialty training after his residency. One of his medical school classmates had applied to NASA and encouraged Sean to do so. After some research, Sean found out that NASA was looking for qualified medical personnel to become candidates for the astronaut program. He decided to apply and began the long application process. After each successful step, he became more excited about the possibility of being selected. He knew only the best of the best would be chosen, but he was willing to compete for the opportunity.

After three months of preliminary testing, he was called to Houston for a five-day interview process. He thought medical school was stressful, but he never experienced anything like the intensity and rigor of that five-day period. After it was over, he was told he would be notified in writing of the final decision in twenty-one days.

When the letter arrived, Sean held it in his hands, closed his eyes and said a brief prayer. Then he ripped open the envelope and read the first sentence. "We are pleased to inform you that you have been selected as a candidate for the next NASA Astronaut Training Program."

Sean yelled to no one in particular, "I made it, I made it!"

He thought he had prepared for the rigors of the training program, but he hadn't realized how well conditioned and trained astronauts were expected to be. The first few weeks had been physically grueling and emotionally draining. Each morning began with strenuous exercise and weight training, followed by a three-mile run. During that initial period Sean wasn't sure if they planned to take a rocket into space or run there.

After physical conditioning, the candidates spent hours either in a classroom or in a simulator, adapting their minds and bodies to function in space. As the only medical person, Sean had additional course work in treating medical conditions in outer space. Despite all the hardships, he had persevered and had even begun to enjoy the challenges.

When Sean arrived at the security area, he was immediately escorted to the planning room. Colonel Gaylord introduced him to several NASA officials and four veteran astronauts in the room. As soon as all of them were seated, one of the NASA officials began speaking.

"This is a top-secret briefing. All of you have the appropriate clearance. There will be no handouts and all written notes will be collected at the end of the meeting. You are not to repeat the contents of this briefing to anyone outside of this room. Is that understood?"

"Yes, sir" chorused through the room.

"Yesterday at 2200 hours we lost communications with the Transverse 7 space station. All efforts to restore communications have been unsuccessful. The station remains in orbit, but we have no contact. We've had specialists analyzing every option, but as of five minutes ago we are no closer to a solution than we were last night. There was a large meteor shower near the space station at approximately the same time, and it's possible that a random meteor struck the station. A meteor hit could cause a communications outage and other possible damage.

"There are twelve people on the Transverse 7 space station. We don't know if any of them are injured. Their lives may depend on how quickly we can resume contact. If we are not successful in restoring communications, we will launch a rescue flight as soon as possible. Fortunately, a routine shuttle mission had been scheduled for three weeks from today, so the rocket is nearly ready. The timetable will be shrunk as much as possible. Preparations for an emergency flight have already begun. Weather conditions are favorable for the next five days. The earliest possible liftoff will be 0500 on Wednesday, four days from today.

"The four astronauts present will pilot the craft and conduct possible rescue operations. Doctor Noel will accompany the crew and provide whatever medical support may be required.

"The five of you are immediately relieved of your current duties and are assigned to the mission. Colonel Gaylord will coordinate the initial preparations. Any specific mission-related questions should be directed to him.

"Are there any questions at this time? If not, this briefing is over."

Sean sat there stunned. Although he had been training hard

for six months, he wasn't sure if he was ready for space travel. Also, he was concerned about what he might find on the space station. Twelve lives may depend on how effective he would be as a medical provider.

The next seventy-two hours were extremely hectic. While the other four concentrated on the operations side of the mission, Sean focused on medical preparation. He participated in briefings and examined medical records and reports from prior space travelers to gain a better understanding of possible problems he might encounter.

The day before the scheduled liftoff, the crew flew from Houston to Cape Kennedy. That night Sean had difficulty sleeping. He had prepared for this mission as best he could in the short period of time. The astronauts with whom he was flying all had prior experience in space. Despite the preparations and safeguards, he was worried. There was always a chance of error, a possible mishap. He tried not to think of the danger, but rather focus on the people who might need his help.

He must have fallen asleep because he had to be awakened at 0230 for a light breakfast, final instructions and donning the space suit. The flight was a go.

After a final check of their space suits, the five of them rode the elevator to the shuttle mounted on top of the rocket. Although they would do nothing until the rocket boosters lifted them beyond the earth's atmosphere, they were going through a checklist to prepare for their roles once they were in space. Suddenly the shuttle door was slammed shut and they were alone in the spacecraft. Each crew member buckled up for the journey.

As the countdown reached T minus twenty seconds, Sean could feel the roar of the rocket engines. He glanced around at the others and they all seemed focused on the mission ahead of them. When the countdown reached ten, the engines were so loud, the shuttle was shaking. Sean closed his eyes and clenched the armrests of his seat.

"FIVE, FOUR, THREE, TWO, ONE, LIFTOFF! WE HAVE A LIFTOFF!"

He felt the rocket rise up from the launch pad. Above the roar, he heard his dad's voice. "Seanny! Seanny! Are you still with us? You look like you're really out there in space."

Sean opened his eyes and stared at his father sitting across from him on the patio. After a brief moment he said, "Dad, you don't know how right you are. I guess the extra schooling is making you smarter."

Noel's Story

It was three weeks before Christmas
And all through this home,
There was just too much happening
To be put in a poem.

Noel and her sister, Alexis, were in their rooms getting ready to visit Santa. Their mom had picked out special Christmas outfits for them to wear. While dressing, Noel was thinking about all the fun things she would do between now and Christmas.

Dad, Alexis and she were going to cut a Christmas tree tomorrow while Riley was sleeping. Dad wanted to surprise Riley and put the tree up before he woke up from his nap. After the tree was secure in the stand, the family would decorate it with their special ornaments.

At school her class had started to practice for the Christmas program. Noel had a big part in the play. Dad said he would video the performance so all her cousins could watch it when they visited Grandma's house.

Mom told Noel she could help bake some cookies this year. Noel liked working in the kitchen, and being asked to help with Christmas cookies made her feel older.

Noel was excited about another special treat this year. Grandma invited Noel to go with her to a performance of the Nutcracker ballet. Since she started dance classes, Noel had fantasized about being a ballerina. In her dream she was on stage in a beautiful costume dancing in front of a live audience. Her parents were in the front row watching intently as she twirled and pirouetted on stage. When she finished her dance, the crowd burst into applause as she took her bows.

Her reverie was interrupted by her dad's shouts. "Are you girls ready? Santa's busy this time of year and he can't wait forever."

Noel and Alexis hurried downstairs, grabbed their coats and jumped in the van. On the way, the girls decided they wanted to sit together on Santa's lap. Since sitting on Santa's lap had been an issue in the past, Dad readily agreed to that suggestion.

After waiting in line, their turn finally arrived. Noel clung to her dad as he lifted her up on Santa's lap. Both girls were nervous, but Santa charmed them with his comments. "I don't think I've seen two prettier sisters in long time."

He started talking to Alexis first. While she was talking, Noel kept thinking about what she was going to say to Santa. Finally Santa turned to her.

"What's your name, little girl?" asked Santa.

"Noel," she said quietly.

"That's a great name, especially for this time of year," said Santa, "because *Noël* means Christmas in French. Noel, what would you like for Christmas?"

"I would like something that'll make me happy," responded Noel without thinking. Noel was surprised at what she had said.

Santa looked puzzled for a moment but then asked, "Is there a special toy that will make you happy?"

"I don't know. I want an American Girl doll, but I don't know if that will make me happy. Mom says sharing with others will make me a happier girl."

"That's good advice," said Santa. "If everyone shared some of their things with others, this would be a happier place to live. My suggestion is follow your mother's advice. Do something nice for someone this Christmas season. You'll have a special feeling knowing that you made someone else happy. Remember whose birthday we celebrate at Christmas."

Noel listened intently and then whispered something in Santa's ear.

"I'll be happy to do that for you, Noel. That's a kind and generous suggestion."

Then Santa turned to both girls. "Thank you for coming and have a merry Christmas."

Dad took a picture of the girls with Santa, and the visit was over.

As Noel walked away, she thought about what Santa had said. When Dad asked her what she had whispered in Santa's ear, Noel smiled and said it was a secret between her and Santa.

On Christmas morning Noel ran down the stairs and peeked at the Christmas tree. The lights glowed and the ornaments glistened. Presents beckoned the kids to open them.

As the family gathered around the tree, Noel spotted a shiny red envelope with her name on it. "Dad, could I open that envelope first?"

"Sure," Dad answered. But he wasn't sure who had put the envelope under the tree.

When Noel tore open the envelope, there was a letter inside. She unfolded the letter and noticed the fancy writing. She eagerly read the message.

Dear Noel,

I kept thinking about your secret request after you left me a few weeks ago. It was so extraordinary, it made me happy for the rest of the week. I'm glad there are girls like you trying to make Christmas a wonderful time for others who may not be as fortunate as you. I hope knowing you did something kind for someone else does bring you happiness.

S

In a different part of the city, another little girl woke up on Christmas morning. Her parents had cautioned her not to expect many presents this year. They told her Santa was very busy and they hadn't been able to help him much because Dad was out of work.

Despite knowing there wouldn't be many presents, she

43

bounded out of bed. After all, it was Christmas Day. Her parents were in the kitchen and they both hugged her as she came through the door. After eating breakfast, she asked if she could open presents. Again, they cautioned her about not having many presents.

When they went into the other room, the little girl saw a large present under the tree. She looked closely and saw her name on the package. There was a shiny red envelope taped to the wrapping. She picked up the envelope and tore it open. Inside there was a note with fancy writing.

This present is for you. It was a suggestion from another little girl with a pretty name. She wanted to do something nice for someone and asked if I could help her. She believes the real meaning of Christmas is in sharing and doing nice things for other people.

Remember this gift. Someday you will be able to do something special for someone else. That is how you can thank the little girl with the pretty name for her kindness. I hope you enjoy the doll.

S

The little girl ripped open the wrapping on the large present. When she opened the box, she saw an American Girl doll inside. It was the gift she really wanted this Christmas. She was afraid to ask for it because of what her parents had told her. As she hugged each of them, she saw her father reach down and pick up the note. He read it and handed it to his wife. The parents looked at each other in amazement.

Thad's Story

Thad was a boy on a mission. As soon as the girls' soccer game started, he waved to his parents and headed for the trees and pond. His two older sisters were playing, and his parents were on the sidelines. He had seen a frog near the little pond last week and he had made plans all week on how he was going to catch it. If he was successful, the frog would make a good pet.

Before the game, Thad told his mom that he was going to look for something near the trees. She cautioned him, "Don't go too far. You know how you lose track of time."

As he hurried forward, Thad kept his head down so he could spot the frog if it wandered from the pond. When he reached the trees, Thad thought he saw something move. He slowed to a walk because he didn't want to scare the frog if it was nearby. Approaching the edge of the pond, Thad spotted the object of his search. The little frog was sunning itself.

When the frog heard Thad approaching, it began to jump away. It didn't go directly for the water but hopped into some thick underbrush. Thad realized he had forgotten to bring a cup or something to catch the frog. He didn't think he could catch it with his bare hands. Even if he did, he wasn't sure he wanted to carry the frog all the way back to the soccer field. He decided to go back and get a cup to catch the frog.

Returning to the game, he walked over to the water cooler and picked up a cup. He saw his mom and waved to her. She smiled and waved back. With the cup in his hand, he headed back toward the pond.

Thad hurried to the spot where he had seen the frog, but it wasn't there. He began to wander further and further into the woods. He thought he saw something near the tall grass so he headed in that direction. When he reached the spot, he found nothing. He continued to wander and search.

Coming to an open space, Thad stopped to look around. Tall grass and cattails swayed gently in front of him. He thought, *That would be a perfect place for a frog to hide.* He began to creep slowly, trying not to make a sound

He was searching when he spotted something colorful trapped in the grass. Thad bent over to get a closer look. It was a large, blue-green feather with a white, fluffy plume near the base of the quill. Thad carefully picked up the feather and held it up to the sun. The sunlight glowed through the feather. He tossed it in the air and watched it flutter back to the ground.

What if this is a magic feather? he asked himself.

His dad had read him a story about a young Indian boy who found a special feather. When the boy wore it on his head, it gave him special powers. Thad wondered if this feather had any special powers for him. He wanted to wear this feather, but he didn't have a headband or anything else to hold it on his head. He took off his belt and tried putting it on his head, but the belt fell around his shoulders. He didn't want to put it in his pocket because it might break and all the magic would leak out.

Thad began waving the feather around and pretending it could make him fly. He twisted and turned and ran in a circle. He flapped his arms and tried to launch himself into the air. He pictured himself soaring in the sky like a hawk and watching everything on the ground. He would hold on to his feather and let it take him to faraway places.

Thad had an idea. If this were a magic feather, it might carry him to a special place where dinosaur bones were buried. There was nothing Thad wanted to do more than to find a dinosaur bone. Then he could dig up the bone and have his picture in the paper for his great discovery.

Thad became excited about this possibility. *Maybe dinosaurs still lived somewhere. They might be hiding from all the people in the world. I'm going to find their hiding place with my magic feather. Then I could have a dinosaur for a pet. It would have to be a small one so it could stay in the barn.*

Suddenly, the little frog didn't matter because he was going to find a different pet.

Thad began talking to the feather. "Magic feather, can you take me to a place where dinosaurs are buried?"

Even though there was no response to his question, Thad wasn't discouraged. He looked around and decided he would begin his search for dinosaur bones right where he was sitting. This was where he found the feather. Maybe that's what the feather was telling him.

He looked around for a stick so he could begin. He realized he would probably need a shovel to dig a hole big enough for a dinosaur bone, but he wanted to get started right away. He walked towards the trees and began looking for a stick big enough to dig a hole.

He spotted a broken limb and grabbed it. It was taller than he was so he had to hold it with two hands. However, it broke into small pieces when he tried to dig with it. After a few minutes he found another branch that still had some leaves attached to it. It was about the right size, so he picked off the leaves. It didn't break when he scratched the ground. He selected a spot near a tree stump, put the feather on the stump and began to make a hole in the ground with the stick.

Thad was so preoccupied with what he was doing, he wasn't aware of the time. He was busy digging when he heard his dad calling his name. He stopped and called back. His dad must not have heard him because he heard his name again. Finally, after several shouts from Thad, he saw his family coming toward him. Everybody was shouting and running. When Thad saw his mom and dad, he could see they were upset.

"Thad, why did you wander so far away from the soccer field?" asked his dad. "We were worried when we couldn't find you after the game. You know you're supposed to tell us where you're going before you leave."

Thad tried to explain how he began by looking for a frog and then found a magic feather. He started to tell them about digging up the dinosaur bones, but no one was listening to him.

Finally, his dad asked, "Thad, what would have happened if we weren't able to find you?"

Thad looked at his dad and said, "I wasn't lost. Besides, I knew you would find me."

"How can you be so sure?" responded his Dad.

"Dad," said Thad seriously, "if you didn't find me, there would be no one to tell stories at dinner."

His dad shook his head, put his arm around Thad and began heading for the van. After a few steps, Thad broke away and ran back to the tree stump. He grabbed the feather and turned back toward his father.

The dinosaur bones would have to wait for another day.

Matthew's Story

It was Christmas morning. Presents and wrappings were all over the family room. Christopher and Andrew, Matthew's older brothers, had started playing one of their new games when Mom reached under the tree and pulled out a small present.

"Matthew, this is for you. I think you're old enough to learn how to tell time, so I got you something to help you out."

She handed the package to Matthew. He ripped off the paper and opened the box. It was a Backyard Baseball watch. The face of the watch was a picture of a baseball diamond with bases where the 3, 6 and 9 would normally be and a home plate instead of the 12. The hands of the watch were two different-size baseball bats.

Matthew jumped up and gave his mom a big hug.

"Can I put it on right now?" he asked.

"Yes, you may. But you have to promise me you'll take care of it and not lose it."

"I'll take care of it, I promise."

His mom helped him get it out of the box and showed him how to put it on his left wrist. Matthew stared at his watch.

"Now I'm going to learn how to tell time!" he proclaimed. "I can't wait to wear it to school and show my teacher and everyone in the class."

The next week was a blur. After their own Christmas there was the special late Christmas at Grandma and Grandpa's with his aunts, uncles and cousins. He proudly wore his new gift every day for everyone to admire. Whenever someone asked him what time it was, he answered, "I'm still learning, but this watch is gonna help."

Uncle Greg asked Matthew, "Did your watch come with a set of instructions on how to use it?"

Matthew laughed. He knew Uncle Greg was teasing him.

Every night he carefully took off his watch and placed it on his nightstand before getting into bed. He was very protective of it and didn't want anything to happen to it.

Christmas vacation came to an end, and the three boys prepared to return to school. They packed their backpacks with their books, papers and other school supplies. Matthew was excited to show his teacher and classmates his new watch.

Matthew got up early for school. He dressed quickly and made sure he put on his watch.

When the bus arrived at school, he grabbed his backpack, waved good-bye to his brothers and quickly headed to his classroom. When he entered the room, he saw a large sign welcoming the class back from Christmas vacation. He was busy saying hello to his friends and showing off his Christmas present when Mrs. Hansen asked everyone to take their seats because she had a special announcement.

"Principal Hanold is so pleased with the progress this class is making, he wants to reward your efforts. He said we can have a special mini Olympics in the gym next Wednesday afternoon with treats afterwards. I'll split the class into two groups, and you'll compete against each other in different contests. The winning team at the end of five events will be the first ones to get the treats after we return to the classroom."

Christian raised his hand and asked, "What kind of contests will we be having?"

Mrs. Hansen smiled and said, "You'll have to wait until Wednesday to find out. I'll give you a couple of clues. All the events will involve physical activity, and everyone will participate."

Matthew was excited with this news. He liked playing games and he liked competing. To be able to do both during school was great. Matthew was so focused on the good news he forgot to show Mrs. Hansen his watch. It was almost lunch time when he remembered to show it to her.

She asked, "Are you able to tell time with your watch?"

"Not yet."

"Don't worry. Later this year we'll have a unit on telling time the old-fashioned way. Your new watch will help you learn."

When Matthew came home from school that afternoon, he told his mom about the special mini Olympics. "We're going to play games in the gym all Wednesday afternoon because the principal said we're doin' so good in school."

Mom rolled her eyes and responded, "I'm sure he said you were doing *well* in school."

After his brothers heard about the special gym day, they kidded Matthew about how easy kindergarten was getting. "We never had special gym days when we were in kindergarten."

Matthew smiled, "Maybe your classes weren't as smart as mine."

After lunch on Wednesday, Mrs. Hansen divided the class into two groups and took them to the gym. "I will coach one team and Mrs. Wentworth will coach the other team."

Matthew and a few of his friends were on Mrs. Wentworth's team. Before the activities started, Mrs. Wentworth gathered her team around her. "I want you to work together. Teamwork will be important in these events. Enjoy the challenge and do your best."

For the first event each coach lined up her team on opposite sides of a blue chalk line that was drawn on the gym floor. A long rope with a flag tied around the middle of the rope laid next to them. Two orange cones sat about six feet apart from each other on opposite sides of the chalk line.

Mrs. Hansen started the festivities. "This event will be a tug of war. Everyone on each team has to grab hold of the rope. The object is to pull the other team across the chalk line and have the flag move past the cone on your side of the line. When I blow the whistle, pick up the rope and start pulling."

After a few minutes of struggling, Mrs. Hansen's team began to slowly pull the others across the line. Despite pleas from Mrs.

Wentworth's team to pull harder, the flag edged past the cone and Mrs. Hansen blew a whistle. "My team is the winner and gets ten points."

Mrs. Hansen's team shouted and cheered.

While Mrs. Wentworth positioned two sets of four cones on the floor, Mrs. Hansen introduced the next game. "The second event is a relay. I want both teams to line up single file behind this line on the gym floor. Each team member has to zigzag as fast as you can around the outside of four cones positioned on the floor, touch the line at the other end of the gym, and run back through the same cones. When you're finished, you have to slap the hand of the next player in line before that player can begin. If someone misses a cone, I will blow the whistle, and that person has to go back and run around the cone. The team that finishes first will be the winner. Now watch Mrs. Wentworth. She's going to demonstrate how to run through the cones."

After the demonstration, Mrs. Hansen blew the whistle and the first person from each squad began to run around the cones. It was close, but one of the students on Mrs. Hansen's team took a tumble and Matthew's team was able to hold the lead and win the event. Mrs. Wentworth's team yelled enthusiastically as they pulled even in the point count.

The third event was a Nerf football toss. Each team member had one turn to throw the football as far as he or she could throw it. But it had to land between two narrow boundaries in order to count. The longest throw between the boundaries won for that team.

When it was Matthew's turn, Mrs. Hansen's team had the lead on a throw by Christian. Matthew grabbed the football, took three steps and threw a long spiral that sailed at least ten feet beyond Christian's throw. Christian's team had two remaining competitors, but neither was able to beat Matthew's throw. Mrs. Wentworth's team won and added ten more points to their total. Matthew's teammates slapped him on the back while they waited for the next event.

This time Mrs. Wentworth did the introduction. "This will be a basketball passing contest. I want each team to line up facing the other team. When the whistle blows, the task is for each team member to hand a basketball to the person next to you. The last person in line then passes the ball back to the next person. The team who returns the ball first to the person who started will be the winner. But, if the ball hits the ground, you have to start over. Are there any questions?"

The teams stood in a line facing each other. As the whistle tweeted, both teams quickly passed the ball down the line. As the ball started back, Matthew's team had a slight lead. Everyone in both lines began shouting at their teammates to hurry up and move the ball. As Ben prepared to receive the ball, he glanced at the line across from him. In that instant, Allison handed him the ball. It trickled off his fingers and fell. Matthew's team groaned as the other team continued to pass the ball successfully back to the head of the line.

Mrs. Hansen's team won easily and received ten points. After four events the score was tied.

Mrs. Wentworth announced the final event. "We are going to have a two-inning kickball game. Each team member will bat once in each half inning. If you successfully reach base, you may advance bases on succeeding players' kicks and try to score a run. The normal rules of kickball will apply except for the number of outs in each half inning. If someone on the opposing team hits you with the ball and you're not on a base, you will be out. The team with the most runs after two innings will be the winner. Mrs. Hansen and I will pitch and umpire for our own team."

In the first inning both teams were sloppy and not many outs were recorded. When Matthew came up in the top of the second inning, his team led by three runs and had two guys on base. He gave a mighty kick to the rolling ball and sent it sailing over the outfielder's head. The ball banged off the gym wall. By the time the outfielder retrieved the ball and threw it back to the infield, three more runs scored.

Matthew's team took the field for the last half inning with a six-run lead. Mrs. Hansen's squad fought back. They scored five runs and had runners on second and third as the last player came to the plate. She kicked a hard grounder to Gustavo. The ball bounced off his leg and ricocheted into right field. Both runners scampered home. Victorious screams could be heard all the way to the principal's office.

Matthew was upset his team had lost. As he began walking out of the gym, he noticed Gustavo was still standing where he had missed the ball. Matthew turned and went back. Gustavo looked like he was ready to cry. Matthew put his hand on Gustavo's shoulder. "Don't worry. It took a bad hop. We'll get a treat anyway. Come on, I'll walk with you back to the room."

Mrs. Wentworth observed the two boys leaving the gym. She called out to them. "Nice job, boys. You played hard."

Then she looked at Matthew. "Matthew, you're a good teammate, but an even better friend."

On the bus ride home, Matthew was still stewing about the kickball game. As he sat in his seat, he glanced at his watch. It wasn't moving. He had worn it during the afternoon's activities. *What else could go wrong? Mom's going to be really upset. This is turning out to be the worst day of my life.*

When he got off the bus with his brothers, he wanted to run up to his room and bury his head in his pillow. Instead he walked into the house and waited for his mom's greeting. She was in the kitchen.

"Hi boys! How was school? There's a snack for everyone on the counter."

Then she saw her youngest son. "Matthew, what's wrong? You look so sad. I thought today was going to be a fun day for you. What happened?"

"It was fun, but our team lost." He told her about the different events. When he got to the kickball game, he mentioned how sad Gustavo was after he missed the ball.

"I tried to help him after the game, but he was pretty upset. I thought he was going to cry. Mrs. Wentworth told me I was a good teammate and friend. Then . . . something else happened. On the way home I looked at my watch and it wasn't working.

I'm sorry, Mom. I didn't mean to break it. I don't know what happened."

"Oh, Matthew." Mom crouched down, wrapped her arms around her boy and gave him a big squeeze.

"I am a little upset about the watch, but not with you. It should not have stopped working just because you were active. We'll get it fixed or replaced. I am really proud of the way you tried to comfort Gustavo. He needed a friend and you were there for him. That's more important to me than you learning how to tell time."

Alexis's Story

The girls were hunched over, looking at the stones that edged Grandma's driveway. Occasionally they would pick up one and hold it up to the sun to see if it would sparkle. Alexis, Noel and their cousin, Nicole, were dressed for the late fall afternoon. A brisk wind blew their hair, but they weren't paying any attention to the weather. They were searching for a special stone, one that captured the sunlight and sparkled like the rings on their moms' fingers.

Wandering away from the other two girls, Lexi began searching in different places. She thought to herself, *If I find a special stone, it might be magical. I would wish to live in a castle high on a hill and wear long, flowing gowns with headdresses to match every outfit.*

She began looking around the red maple that produced large crimson leaves. Now the tree looked cold and bare without its summer cloak. When nothing caught her eye near the tree, she wandered back toward the garden. The other two girls got discouraged and started to play on the patio.

Lexi was about to give up her search when she spotted a small oval stone half buried in the dirt near the garden. It had streaks of red and blue marbling throughout its cream color. Lexi picked it up and felt its smooth surface. It didn't look magical, but it was pretty. She rubbed off the dirt and held it up to the sun. There was no sparkle, but it felt warm in her hand. Just then Noel called to Alexis to come and play with them. Lexi stuck the stone in her coat pocket and ran to join the other girls.

After supper at Grandma's, Alexis and Noel gathered their

belongings and gave them to their dad. When everything was packed, they kissed their grandparents and hopped in the van. On the way home, their mom asked the girls, "What were you looking for in the yard?"

Alexis was half asleep as she heard Noel talk about trying to find a special stone. Alexis closed her eyes. As she began to fade, she remembered what was in her pocket. She reached her hand inside to check if it was still there. As her fingers touched the stone, she again felt the warmth that she had felt that afternoon. She began to slowly rub the stone and felt a warm sensation come over her. She wrapped herself in this comfortable glow and fell asleep.

When Alexis opened her eyes, she was standing in a large field with beautiful wild flowers growing everywhere. The sun was shining and the sky was a crystal blue. She looked around but didn't see anyone else. Despite being alone, she was not afraid. Alexis began dancing in the field, spinning and twirling in the breeze. When she smelled the beautiful fragrance from the flowers, Alexis decided to pick some to make a bouquet for her mom. So intent on gathering the flowers, she didn't notice what was on the horizon.

Then she looked up and saw the castle high on a hill. A bright light surrounded the building. She forgot about the flowers and began walking toward the mirage. Alexis didn't know how long she traveled, but she was now close enough to see a tall iron fence in front of the castle.

As she paused to consider what to do next, a huge gate swung open. She saw a woman standing in a courtyard, waving for her to come in. Even though she was being cautious, Alexis felt drawn to the castle.

Walking through the entrance, Lexi got a better look at the person who was waving to her. She was young with a pretty smile, dressed in a long, flowing yellow gown with a matching crown and veil. She held out her hand, and Alexis noticed the sparkling rings on her fingers.

"Welcome, Alexis," she said in a lyrical voice. "My name is

Angelina. You are entering a special place. Its proper name is Il Piccolo Castello, but most people call it the Happy Place. Inside these walls you can do whatever you want from morning till night. You can sing and dance and play games. You can dress up in long, flowing gowns and very tall hats. You won't have to do any chores."

Angelina took Lexi's hand and together they walked into the castle. Alexis was excited to be in such a place, but all she could do was smile. As they walked down a large hallway with a huge candelabra hanging from the ceiling, Lexi heard their footsteps echo off the brick walls.

Angelina began explaining the unique features of the castle. "We have special rooms for different activities. For example, the room on our left is for board and video games. Alexis, do you enjoy playing any games?"

"My family likes to play *Apples to Apples* and *Clue.*"

"I'm sure we have those games. On the right we have a dance studio and a music room called the Chamber."

"Oh, I love to dance," said Alexis. "I've already started lessons. Someday I hope to be a ballerina."

"Let me quickly tell you about some of the other rooms. The stuffed animals reside in the Zoo and the dolls are in the Doll House. Toy cars and trucks are in the Show Room and building blocks are stored in the Carpenter's Shed. The Locker Room has every kind of ball you can imagine and, of course, the Dressing Room has countless outfits with matching jewelry. You can play wherever you want.

"I have to leave you for a short time," Angelina said, "but I'll be back."

Before she left, Angelina gave Alexis a tiny bell. "Ring it whenever you want anything."

As soon as she was alone, Alexis rushed back to the dance studio. She was a little timid as she approached the large room. Angelina said she could play anywhere she wanted, but now she was by herself.

Alexis peaked into the room. It was empty. She tiptoed

through the door and heard music. Overcoming her shyness, Alexis started to dance. She glided and twirled in time to the music. As the music changed, Alexis began to perform ballet. She got up on her toes and stepped and pirouetted like a ballerina. She thought about her sister. *We could have so much fun dancing and playing in this room.*

Finally, she tired of dancing and began exploring this magical place. The next room she entered was the Chamber. There was every musical instrument she could imagine. Alexis sat at the piano and began to play. She surprised herself. She was playing a real song. She played another and then a third. All of them sounded pleasant. Then she spotted a drum set in the corner. She walked over, sat on a stool, picked up the sticks and began slowly tapping the instrument. As she gained a little confidence she started to beat out a rhythm.

Next Alexis picked up a trumpet. After a few attempts, she was able to make some sounds. She started high-stepping around the room pretending she was in a marching band. She marched right out of that room and into the Dressing Room.

Alexis put down the trumpet and gazed at all the dresses and matching accessories. She picked out a long, flowing pink dress with a matching crown and tried them on. She put on some jewelry and pranced in front of the mirror. She pretended she was the kind lady welcoming new people to the castle.

Then she selected a sapphire dress with matching shoes and some sparkling jewelry. This time she played like she was Cinderella at the ball gracefully dancing across the floor with her pretend prince. After spending more time in the dress-up room, Alexis was getting hungry. She remembered what Angelina had said and began to ring her bell. Suddenly a little man in a bright blue costume with a matching tall hat appeared in the Dressing Room.

"How may I assist you, my child?"

Alexis asked, "May I please have something to eat?"

"Of course! You may have anything you want. What would you like?"

"I think I'd like some chocolate chip cookies and a glass of milk."

"Very good. I'll be back promptly with your milk and cookies."

While she waited for her snack, Alexis sat at a table and wondered about this place. *I'm having a great time, but something's not right.*

Before the food arrived, Angelina returned and sat with Alexis.

"Are you enjoying yourself?" asked Angelina.

"Yes, I'm really having fun. But, I don't know, something's missing. I don't have anyone to play with. I think I'd rather be back with my family."

Angelina smiled. "I'm glad you feel that way. Having all this stuff is nice, but it can never replace family. Now I'm going to ask you to do something for me. Close your eyes and think about something very special. When you open them, you'll have a surprise."

Alexis did as she was instructed. She closed her eyes and thought of Christmas morning. When she opened them, she looked around and saw Noel asleep next to her. Her mom and dad were in the front seat. The van was turning into their driveway.

Her mom turned around and whispered to the girls, "We're home."

Alexis smiled.

Abby's Story

Abby sat on the bank of the pond across the street from her house. Normally Abby was full of energy and ready for any new adventure. She played baseball with her brothers, swam in the family's aboveground pool and rode her bike around the neighborhood. She liked walking through the field to her friend Katie's house, even though she could barely see over the tall grass. She considered this area her own private nature park.

This afternoon, Abby was satisfied with sitting near the water and observing. She watched a frog dive into the water, causing ripples on the surface. Now that she was in kindergarten, Abby didn't have as much time to play outside. Even though she really enjoyed school, Abby missed the freedom of being able to roam around and spend time at the pond.

Each season the pond presented new enjoyment. In the spring the snapping turtles came out, and the DNR stocked the big pond with walleye fingerlings. In late June, George, the snowy white egret, made his appearance and took up residence near the pond. There were frogs and turtles to catch and ticks to avoid. In the fall geese made their big splash and used the pond as a stopping point on their trips to elsewhere. The trees along the banks provided a palette of fall colors reflecting in the water. In the winter nature painted a stark picture on its white canvas. The pond froze and was great for ice-skating, hockey and even cross-country skiing.

As Abby sat gazing at the water, her mind wandered. *I can't wait until I'm as old as my sister, Meghan, and can do the things that Meghan does. I can't wait until I'm in middle school. If I could find a way to speed up everything, I could accomplish things with far less waiting.*

She thought about the future. *What would it be like to be the same age as Meghan? Imagine how much fun we could have if we went to middle school and high school together.*

She closed her eyes, crossed her fingers and wished real hard that she was as old as Meghan. She squeezed her eyes tightly and tried to picture herself and Meghan as the same age. As she sat with her eyes closed she felt something was changing.

Abby wasn't sure what happened, but when she opened her eyes, she didn't recognize any of her surroundings. She was still wearing her same clothes, but everything else was different. Gone were her house and the pond. Instead she found herself in an area that looked like a farm. Abby closed her eyes again and tried to return to the pond. She squeezed her eyes shut to make this go away. She was no longer concerned about being the same age as Meghan; she just wanted to be home.

With her eyes closed, she chanted to herself, "Please take me home, please take me home."

She opened her eyes and peeked at her surroundings. Nothing had changed. She was still in the same place. Abby sat on the ground and started to cry. With tears rolling down her cheeks, Abby looked around. There was no one to help her; she had to help herself. Once she made that decision, her sense of adventure began to take over. She wiped her eyes and decided to find out where she was and then find a way home.

Abby looked around, saw a dirt path and started walking. After a few minutes she saw an old house in the distance. As she approached the house, she saw a woman working in a garden. Abby noticed the old-fashioned clothes the woman was wearing. She wore a long dress and had a hat covering her hair.

The person looked up, spotted Abby and waved. Abby returned the wave and saw the person was not a woman, but a girl about Meghan's age.

The girl stopped working, took off her hat and said, "Hello. What's your name? Are you visiting someone around here?"

Abby was a bit unsure where to start so she just said, "I'm Abby. Could you tell me where I am?"

"You're on the Johnson farm."

Abby had several questions she wanted to ask the other girl, but decided to get more information before telling anyone about her situation.

The girl introduced herself. "I'm Julia. I live here. My mom and dad have been farming this land for more than twenty years."

Abby asked, "How old are you?"

"I'm eleven and I'm in fifth grade."

Abby responded, "My sister's almost twelve and she's in the sixth grade. My brother's in the fifth grade but he's still ten."

Not yet ready to tell Julia about her predicament, Abby just stood there not knowing what to say or do next.

Julia looked closely at Abby. "You're not from 'round here. Your clothes are so different. You're so young. Are you by yourself? Are you lost?"

Abby chose to answer the last question. "Yah, kinda."

"Can I help? Let me finish diggin' these potatoes, then we'll talk."

Abby watched as Julia dug up some potatoes and put them in a sack. She noticed the old-fashioned boots Julia was wearing. When Julia finished, she put her hat back on, grabbed the potato sack and began to walk.

"Come on. While we're walkin', I'll show you some of the farm."

They started toward the barn. "I need to stop at the chicken coop for some eggs."

Abby was a bit timid so she watched from the door. Julia felt around the chickens nesting in the coop. She found some eggs and put them in a large pocket in the front of her dress.

As she came out of the coop, Julia pointed to the fenced area. "That's where we keep the pigs."

Abby looked but didn't see any pigs. She didn't want to get too close to the pig pen. Abby did see several chickens wandering around, stopping every few steps and pecking the ground.

Abby asked, "Are the chickens always allowed to walk around?"

Julia smiled, "Chickens don't wander far from food."

Becoming intrigued with the farm, Abby asked Julia, "How many animals do you have?"

"In addition to the chickens and pigs, we have some cows, but they're in the field grazin'. They'll be returnin' for milkin' in a few hours. We all pitch in with the milkin'."

As they reached the barn, Abby saw piles of hay and several empty stalls. There were a few cats in the barn, but they ran off as soon as they saw Abby.

Under different circumstances, Abby would have enjoyed visiting this farm and learning more about the animals. This could be a wonderful experience, especially this old-fashioned farm. Now, however, Abby was concerned about getting home.

Not really knowing what else to say, Abby asked Julia about her family.

"I live here with my mother, father and two brothers. My folks came from farm families. My brothers want to stay farming, but I'm not sure. It's hard work and there's always chores to do."

As Julia was talking, she looked directly at Abby. "Abby, how old are you? Where did you come from and how did you get here? You're too young to be here by yourself. You don't look like you're from farm people. Your clothes aren't like farm kids wear."

Abby took a deep breath and then blurted out. "I don't know how I got here."

Julia asked, "Who are you visitin'?"

Because Julia seemed friendly and Abby didn't know what else to say, Abby decided to tell her the whole story. "I was sitting at the pond near my house. I closed my eyes and wished that I was as old as my sister. When I opened them, I was here. I don't know how I got here."

Julia looked at her in disbelief. "Abby, I don't know what to say. Your story is so unbelievable, but you're so sincere. Did you fall and hit your head? I think you'd better come in the house and sit down."

As Julia led Abby into the house, Abby looked around in amazement. She was in a large room with a big wooden table and several chairs. There was no carpeting, no television and no appliances.

Julia offered Abby a chair and said, "Sit here. I'm goin' to get my mom."

As Abby sat in the chair, she closed her eyes, dropped her head and clenched her hands together.

She was distracted by a large splash somewhere in the distance. She looked up and saw she was back at the pond. Relieved and thankful, Abby got up and headed to her house. As she walked, she thought about that strange daydream. None of it made sense to her.

Abby couldn't get out of her mind Julia and all her chores. *Maybe growing up quickly might not be so neat after all.*

Valerie's Story

Valerie can be a quiet girl, a very quiet girl. When she's with her cousins, she's as talkative as the others. At home by herself, she plays for hours without making sound. More than once, her mother has had to look for her because she was being so quiet. Her sisters and brother haven't really ever noticed how quiet Valerie is. She's their youngest sister, and they talk for her when necessary.

One morning Valerie was in the family room with her doll, Dolly, watching *Dora* on television. When the show was over, she began talking to her doll the way Dora talked to Boots. "Dolly, I'm the mother and you're the baby. You have to listen to me. It's time for lunch. I'm going to put you in your high chair so I can feed you."

When she was done feeding, Valerie put the doll on her shoulder to burp it.

Tired of playing mother, Valerie started to play school with Dolly. She pretended she was the teacher. She sat Dolly in a chair and tried to teach her the alphabet.

Then she had a strange idea. What if her doll became her real sister? She could be Dolly's older sister. She knew her doll couldn't talk, but that wasn't a problem for Valerie. As she sat on the couch, she began to imagine the fun it would be to have a younger sister. They could share a bedroom and be together every day.

For the rest of the morning, Valerie pretended she and Dolly were sisters. When her mom called Valerie for lunch, the two of

66

them came to the table. Valerie told her mother, "We now have one more girl in the family. I've decided my doll is really my younger sister."

Her mom smiled, shrugged and said, "Welcome, little girl. What would you like for lunch?"

Valerie carefully put Dolly in a separate chair. She insisted her doll have her own plate and glass.

When Frances, Dorielle and Thad got home from school that afternoon, Valerie made her big announcement. "As of right now, Dolly is a member of the family. She'll eat with us, she'll sleep in my bedroom and she'll join in all family activities."

Valerie's sisters smiled at her condescendingly. Frances tried to be receptive. "That's nice, Val. We'll have to remember to include our new sister in all our activities."

Dorielle took a more philosophical approach. "I think we should be open to change in this family. Good idea. Let's give it a try."

Then the older girls ran upstairs to change and begin their after school activities.

Thad reacted quite differently. "Val, that's dumb. You can't be serious. Pretending a doll is a person is ridiculous. Forget it! Everyone will laugh at us. That's just what we need in this family, another girl."

"I'm serious. Besides, who made you the boss of anything?"

Before supper that night, Thad tried to talk to his mom about Valerie's scheme.

"Mom, I have a solution to Val's crazy idea. She's trying to make that doll a member of the family because she doesn't have anyone to play with while we're at school. I think you should have another baby so Val will have somebody."

Thad's mother cocked her head and looked over her glasses at him. Whenever she did that, Thad knew he wasn't going to make any headway with her.

While Thad was trying to talk to his mother, Valerie was in the family room giving Dolly some advice about certain family activities.

"We eat supper as a family so we have to wait until Dad gets home from work. That's why Mom has a snack for the kids when they get home from school. If you have any homework, do it before we eat. Sometimes it's pretty late when we finish. Also, stay away from Thad. He doesn't like our idea."

When she heard her dad's car in the drive, Valerie was the first one to meet him. As he lifted her up for a hug, she began to tell him about her doll becoming a member of the family.

Her father was only half listening and said, "I think that's great. Hello everybody! I'm home."

Thad was entering the kitchen when he heard his dad agree with Valerie. He winced at the prospect of having to treat a doll as a sister.

When Thad finally got a chance to greet him, he whispered into his father's ear, "Dad, we gotta talk quick. Just you and me."

He tried to get his dad to follow him into the dining room, but his father stood in the kitchen talking to his mom and sisters. While Thad was waiting in the dining room, Valerie returned to the kitchen with her doll in her arms.

"Dad, meet the newest member of the family," she said as she held Dolly up for her father to hug. "Since this is the first family meal with Dolly, I think we should make it a party."

Frances played right along with Valerie. "I think a party is a great idea, Val. Can we, Mom, please? We can have soda with supper and cake for dessert? It'll be like a birthday party."

"Slow down," Mom said. "You can have soda, but it's too late to make a cake. I'll come up with something for dessert. Let's get the table set."

"Party hats! We need party hats!" Dorielle blurted out. "I have some left over from my birthday."

Mom headed back into the kitchen with Frances and Valerie. Dorielle ran to her room. Frances shouted, "I'll get the special plate for Dolly!"

When she returned with a bunch of party hats, Dorielle started placing them by each plate at the table. "I'm one short. Dad, I don't have enough hats."

"Maybe I can help you out," Dad responded.

He grabbed a page from the newspaper, folded it into a hat and put it by his plate.

"Now we have enough."

With all this activity going on around him, Thad stood there shaking his head.

After she and Frances finished setting the table, Valerie grabbed a pillow from the family room and put it on a chair. Then she carried Dolly to the table and put her on the pillow. She even had a bib for Dolly.

As Mom brought the food from the kitchen, the rest of the family sat down to eat.

After saying a blessing, Valerie's dad rose in mock solemnity. He raised his glass and proposed a toast. "This is to Dolly. Welcome! It's rare that we get a chance to add to our family. I'm sure you'll become a proud member of this distinguished group. But we have one minor problem. As I look around this table, I am pleased with the names we have chosen for each of our children. I'm afraid the name Dolly doesn't quite measure up. We need to come up with a new name, something more distinguished. This will take some time, much thought and many discussions. In the meantime, let's raise our glasses and toast the newest family member."

Everyone but Thad cheered and clicked their glasses together. Thad sat pinned to his chair.

When the noise died down, Valerie stood up. "I want to say something."

Since Valerie didn't talk very often at dinner, everyone quieted down. Giggling, she said, "Dad, I think Thad should have to come up with at least one suggestion for a name. He's part of this family."

Dad looked at Thad. "Well, Thad, what do you think of Val's suggestion?"

Trying to change the subject, Thad looked around the table. "Why is it always hot at the end of a soccer game?"

He waited for a response. When no one volunteered an answer, he blurted out, "Because all the fans have gone home."

When the groans stopped, Thad raised both hands. "I still think this is ridiculous. But if I have to come with a name, I think we should call it Dummy or Dumb for short. That's because—"

"That's enough, Thad," his mother said. "Don't be a party pooper."

After dinner, Mom brought in a last-minute dessert she put together for the occasion. After cutting a piece for Dolly, she put one candle in the middle. Dad lit the candle and the family sang a chorus of "Happy Birthday."

Later that night as Mom was tucking Valerie and Dolly into bed, she commented on the evening. "That was an enjoyable party, girls. Valerie, you were certainly more chatty than normal. I guess being an older sister has changed you."

Valerie looked at her mom. "I really had fun pretending Dolly was part of the family."

Then she reached up, gave her mom a big hug and whispered in her ear. "Tell Thad he doesn't have to worry about having a doll for a sister. Besides, I like being the youngest in the family. Tomorrow, Dolly will be just a doll again."

Nicole's Story

Nicole was waiting as the school bus headed down the street. When the bus came to a stop, and Pat, the driver, swung the door open, Nicole was up the steps and in her seat before her brothers reached the end of the driveway. Christopher hopped on the bus next and Andrew followed. Matthew came running and timed his jump just before Pat closed the door.

Pat glanced at Nicole and noticed she was wearing a fancy dress and her hair was curled.

"Is today something special? You seem to be in a rush to get to school," Pat said to Nicole as the bus started up again.

Nicole answered, "Today's my day to be the storyteller in our class."

Three weeks ago Nicole had brought home a lesson plan outline from her teacher, Mrs. Gross. The class was beginning a unit on storytelling the following Monday. The purpose was to demonstrate to the children how storytelling can be an enjoyable way of communicating information, learning about others and preserving traditions. The class would focus on developing listening skills. During the unit, the class would hear three different adult storytellers use stories as an entertaining way of presenting their customs and heritage. At the end of each story, the children would talk about the stories and discuss what they learned from the storyteller.

To highlight the learning experience, each student in the class would be expected to tell the class a story about his or her family. It could be a story about a family event or a favorite vacation;

it could be about a single family member or the entire family. It could even be about a family pet or a special stuffed animal. There would be no restriction on the length of the story as long as it related to the storyteller's family.

When her mom read the sheet, the two of them started talking about possible topics Nicole could use for her story. They mentioned several options, including the girls' tea parties with Grandma, being the only girl and leading scorer on a soccer team dominated by boys, or the unpleasant experience of being stung by a bee as she was going to lunch on the first day of school.

"Nicole, one of the challenges will be to pick one story and stick with it throughout your talk," her mom said as they were winding down the conversation.

During the next two weeks Nicole wrestled with the subject matter for her story. Each day when she came home from school, Nicole asked her younger brother, David, to sit and listen to her tell a story.

Each day she told a different story. For a while she thought her story about the family Halloween party in Uncle Greg's barn would be the best. The class would like all the scary stuff. Her mom kept encouraging her to tell the story of how Nicole was Grandma's special at-home helper after Grandma's foot surgery. Nicole even tried to build a story around Uncle Steve's dog, Bucky, and how the dog came to live at Grandma's house.

With all these possibilities, Nicole was struggling to choose just one for her story. When Nicole went to bed each night, her mom would ask, "Have you made a decision about which story you are going to tell the class?"

Each night Nicole would respond, "I'm still trying to decide which one would be the best."

When the big day finally arrived, Nicole's mom had suggested that she wear a special dress for the occasion and helped curl her hair. She even had doughnuts as a breakfast treat for Nicole. As she was giving her a kiss good-bye, Nicole's mom wished her good luck and asked her what story she had decided to tell.

"Are you going to let me in on the secret?" she asked as she helped Nicole on with her coat.

Nicole smiled and said, "I'll tell you and the boys my story at dinner tonight. Until then it's still a surprise."

Somewhat taken back by Nicole's answer, her mom gave Nicole a big hug and watched her race down the drive in front of her brothers.

Then Nicole's mom did something very uncharacteristic. She called Nicole's teacher. She knew Mrs. Gross would be in her classroom before the children arrived. Mrs. Gross answered the call on the second ring.

After identifying herself, she asked, "When will Nicole be telling her story? And would it be okay if David and I came to school and listened to the story from the hall? I don't want to disrupt the class."

Mrs. Gross answered, "Nicole will be telling her story at approximately one thirty, right after recess. It'll be fine if you want to listen. I'll leave the door opened slightly so you can hear her. It'll be our secret."

That afternoon Nicole's mom and David drove to school. They walked straight to Nicole's classroom and stood outside the door. They heard Mrs. Gross quiet the class and call on Nicole to tell her story. Nicole stood before the class with her back to the door.

"Angela and I were sitting together on the bus on the way back from a field trip. We started talking about our families. I told her how much fun it was having four brothers.

"Angela was shocked. 'How can you stand having that many boys around you? You must not have any privacy. You probably never get to choose a TV program or a video. Aren't they always picking on you? I really feel sorry for you. I'm glad I don't have any brothers.'

"I was surprised but not upset by Angela's comments. I thought for a minute before I answered her.

"Angela, you don't understand. I agree that sometimes it's hard to talk at the dinner table because all the boys are talking at the same time. Yes, there are times when my brother Matthew teases me and tries to get me upset. But there are so many other good things that happen because I have my brothers.

"When I started kindergarten, the teachers and the principal knew who I was because of my brothers. When I started to play soccer this fall, I was able to score goals because I had played soccer with my brothers. They showed me how to dribble, pass and kick the ball.

"I was stung by a bee at lunch time on the first day of school. It really hurt. My oldest brother, Christopher, saw me crying and came to help. He ate lunch with me to keep me company.

"I began taking piano lessons early because Christopher and Andrew were already taking them. I met my friend Ashley because Matthew is on the same baseball team as her brother. We played together during their games.

"My big buddy, Julie Ann, is in class with Christopher. She thinks he's pretty smart.

"When I get home after school, I often play with my younger brother, David. Right now I am trying to teach him to make shapes and letters so he will learn them before he goes to school."

"With so many brothers, there is always something happening at home. It's really fun having a large family. Also, my brothers have friends. My Grandma met my Grandpa through one of her brothers. Who knows, I may meet someone through one of my brothers.

"As the bus drove into the school's parking lot, I glanced out the window and saw Andrew standing in front of school. He waved as I got off the bus.

"'Hurry, Nicole, Mom's waiting for us! Tonight's piano night and she came to give us a ride. Christopher and Matthew are already in the van. Give me your backpack so we can run!'

"I turned to Angela, who was right behind me, and said, 'See how nice it is to have brothers looking out for me?'

Nicole returned to her seat and Mrs. Gross stood up from her desk. She looked directly at the slightly opened door and smiled. "Thank you, Nicole, for that story about your brothers. I had Christopher and Matthew in class and they're both very thoughtful boys."

74

Nicole's Mom quietly closed the door to the classroom and began walking with David to the van. She thought about the many possible topics Nicole could have used for her story. She decided Nicole deserved something special for dinner.

Riley's Story

Riley likes when his mom does special things with the kids. Today she is taking him and Molly to the library for story hour while his older sisters are in school. His mom didn't tell Riley she had called the librarian, a family friend, earlier in the week to tell her that she would be bringing her two youngest children to the story hour. The librarian had a special story she had picked out for the next time Riley was at story hour.

After the introduction of the children who are attending this story hour, the librarian announces that she has selected a story titled *Son of Spider-Man*. As the group quiets down and settles in their places, she begins to read.

There are many secrets about the legends of the super heroes. One of the best-kept secrets is that Spider-Man had a son. Because Peter Parker, who is Spider-Man, wanted to safeguard the identity of his child and keep him from danger, he told no one of this blessed event. Mary Jane, the child's mother, understood the gravity of the situation and agreed with Peter that their child's safety had to be their ultimate concern. Mary Jane left the city several months before the child was due. Peter was with her when she had the child, a baby boy, at a small hospital far away from New York City. Only a few people knew of the child's birth and those people didn't know Peter was Spider-Man.

Shortly after the birth of their son, the boy's parents made a most difficult decision. As much as they loved their son, they knew the child would be in constant danger if he remained with them. Also, the presence of a child might somehow compromise Spider-Man's secret identity. After discussing the predicament for several days, they reached a conclusion both of them had dreaded. They knew they had to give up their child for adoption. Once that difficult decision was made, the next step was to find a suitable family for the baby.

Peter and MJ decided the baby should be raised in a family with other children. Since Peter was raised as an only child, he could relate to the loneliness the baby would experience growing up without siblings.

Peter had a close friend, Tom, who knew Peter's secret identity. Tom was married to Fran and had two daughters. Peter knew Tom and Fran were loving parents and his son would be safe with them. They would love the boy as their own and raise him to be a fine young man. Since his friend knew Peter was Spider-Man, he would understand why Peter had to give up his child for the child's safety.

Peter and Mary Jane met with Tom and Fran to talk about their son's safety. Peter explained how he and MJ decided to give up their child to safeguard him from harm. He tried to tell them how difficult this decision was to make, but he knew that they understood because they had children of their own. Finally he asked the most difficult question he ever had to pose.

"Would you adopt our baby and raise him as your son? This is his only chance to have a normal life. If you agree, please promise you will never tell the boy who his real parents are. When he is older, you can tell the boy he was adopted."

Tom and Fran thought they could tell their girls that the baby's parents were unable to care for the baby and they had agreed to adopt the child. Since the girls were still very young, they would not be too inquisitive. Also, they were relocating to a different state in the near future, so no one in the new location would know the baby was not always a member of their family.

After a lengthy discussion, Tom and Fran agreed to the proposal. "We're honored you would trust us with your son. We'll love him and raise him as our own. We promise to keep your secret and tell no one, not even the child, who his real parents are. Both of you will be welcome at any time to visit your child. We would like to ask a favor. We would like to name the baby. We had chosen a name if we ever had a boy. After two girls we're not sure we'll ever have the chance to use the name. This may be our only opportunity. It would be our way of making the baby part of our family."

Peter winced at this request. "I really wanted to name the boy Benjamin after my Uncle Ben. Yet, I understand the commitment both of you are willing to make for our boy. I will agree, with one condition. If I don't think the name is suitable for my son, I can reject it."

The couple agreed to this condition. "The name we have always wanted for a boy," said Tom, "is Riley. In Gaelic the name Riley means valiant or courageous."

After hearing the name and the explanation, Peter concurred. "If the name couldn't be Benjamin, Riley was a very suitable alternative."

Riley grew into a very happy young boy. He loved his parents and his sisters. He enjoyed playing with construction toys and learned to ride a bike. He liked watching television and reading books. He relished working with his dad on different projects and helping his mother with chores around the house.

There was one thing Riley enjoyed doing more than anything else. He loved putting on his Spider-Man outfit and pretending he was Spider-Man. Peter, his dad's friend, had given him the costume for Halloween and it immediately became his favorite pastime.

At first, his mom was apprehensive with the outfit. When she saw how much he enjoyed playing Spider-Man, she became less concerned. Then one day the anxiety reappeared. At bedtime Riley told his mother he was going to be Spider-Man's helper, just as Robin was Batman's helper.

Trying not to show her emotions, his mother told him, "Spider-Man doesn't need any help. He's doing fine as a solo."

She kissed Riley and tucked him in bed. She immediately went downstairs and told her husband about Riley's comments. His first reaction was to dismiss it as a boy's wishful fancy. "Every boy goes through these stages. One week they want to be a super hero. The next week they want to be a fireman or policeman. Then they want to be a baseball or football player. As they grow older they develop different interests and all the wishful fantasies are forgotten."

Months went by and Riley persisted in his ambition of becoming "Boy Riley," Spider-Man's partner. His parents decided they would alert Peter the next time he visited Riley.

When they received a call from Peter a few weeks later saying he and MJ were in town, they told him about Riley's career choice. The four of them decided to meet for dinner and discuss the issue before Peter and MJ visited the children.

After catching up on the activities in their lives since their last trip, they talked about Riley's ambition. Over dessert and coffee, they all agreed on a course of action.

Peter and MJ's visits were special occasions for the three children. Besides the small gifts they received, each child had the opportunity to tell their parents' friends all about what was going on in their lives. Peter would amuse the group with some of the crazy things going on in New York City. The children were allowed to stay up beyond their bed times to prolong the visit.

When it was Riley's turn to talk about what was happening in his life, he proudly announced, "I've made a decision. I'm going to become Spider-Man's partner."

The girls had heard about Riley's plans so they just laughed at his fantasy. The adults responded differently. Peter asked Riley, "Why do you want to be Spider-Man's partner? Aren't you concerned about the danger?"

Riley responded, "Naw. I want to help make the world better by getting rid of bad guys just like Spider-Man."

Instead of treating his reply as childish, Peter answered, "That's quite noble, but you don't have to be Spider-Man's helper to make the world better. People can help others in a variety of ways. Parents who teach their children care and respect benefit society. Healthcare professionals help sick and injured people every day. Churches hold food and clothing drives to feed and clothe poor people. Teachers educate children so they can be better citizens. There are many other large and small ways all of us can make the world a better place."

When Peter finished, Riley nodded his head, but didn't say anything. In bed that night, Riley told his mom, "It would be fun to be Spider-Man's helper, but I might do other things. I'll find some way to help people."

His mom gave him a hug. "I'm confident you'll find a way to make a difference."

On the drive home from the library, Riley's mom asked him, "What did you think of the story the librarian read?"

Riley responded, "I didn't know Spider-Man had a son named Riley."

His mom persisted. "Wasn't there anything else about the story you liked?"

Riley thought for a moment. "I thought it was a good thing the boy wanted to do something to help others."

With a slight nod and a silent prayer of thanks, his mom knew the message in the story had been received.

David and Samuel's Story

David is tall, Samuel is not; David has light hair, Samuel has dark hair; David has blue eyes, Samuel has brown eyes. Despite their physical differences, David and Samuel are more like brothers than cousins. Although David is six months older, the two have developed a friendship bond at a young age that many biological brothers do not achieve in their lifetimes.

The two have many things in common. Both like marbles, playing outside and going to the zoo. They have budding interests in sports, enjoy playing on the computer and teasing their sisters. Each is apprehensive of anyone dressed in an oversized costume, like Bernie Brewer or Monkey Joe. Neither would be the first in line to go down to the basement by himself or go into a dark room alone. If Dr. Seuss were describing this pair, he might be tempted to call them Wimp 1 and Wimp 2.

They enjoy each other's company and look forward to being together. When the two of them see one another they embrace and roll around like two playful bear cubs.

One day last fall Samuel was outside with his dad. While his father was tending to outside chores, Samuel was wandering in the woods at the back of their property. All his sisters were inside, so he had the backyard to himself. He was walking along, shuffling his feet like boys do. As he kicked through a small pile of leaves, he spotted an envelope. He picked up the wet envelope, opened it and carefully unfolded the soggy paper inside. Samuel saw words on the top of the page, a diagram, tiny pictures and more words on the rest of the document. The diagram had dashes connecting several objects and a big X near the bottom of the paper.

His imagination took over. *Was this a treasure map? How did it get in our backyard? Maybe the people who lived in the house before us hid it. Could this map lead me to a buried treasure?*

Samuel looked around to see if anyone was watching him. His first impulse was to run and show it to his dad. Then he had another thought. *Wouldn't it be fun to keep it a secret and show it to David?* Since David was in school, Samuel was confident David was learning how to read. Maybe together they might be able to read the words. Once they knew what the map said, they might find a treasure.

Samuel didn't know where to hide his discovery until he could show it to David. He thought about putting it back where he found it. But what if the wind blew the leaves away? The map could blow away as well. Besides, he wasn't sure when David would be over since he had school every day. Samuel carefully refolded the paper, put it inside his jacket and ran toward the house. He had to find a hiding place for the map until he could show it to David. As he entered the garage, Samuel quickly looked around for a secure spot. He decided to hide it in a planter that would not be used until next spring.

Samuel rarely used the phone. He decided this was a special occasion and asked his mom if he could call David. His mom said yes and punched in the phone number for him.

****

David had an after-school routine since he started school. He rode the school bus home with Matthew and Nicole. After arriving home, he immediately told his mom about his day. Then he had a snack and began his homework.

David had finished discussing his class newsletter with Mom and was coloring when the phone rang. Mom answered the phone and handed it to David. After David said hello, Samuel blurted out, "I found something special in our backyard and want to show it to you. When can you come over? I can't tell you what it is over the phone because it's a secret. I hid it in the garage. Don't tell anyone."

Samuel had aroused David's curiosity. After the phone call David asked his mom, "When can I go to Samuel's house?"

Mom said, "Gabriella's birthday is next Sunday, so you'll see Samuel then. Is anything wrong? Samuel normally doesn't call you."

David responded, "Samuel wants to show me something. I can't tell you anything else." He thought to himself, *because I don't know anything else.*

Moms seem to know when not to question their kids further, so nothing more was said about the phone call.

When David was in bed that night, he tried to imagine what Samuel had found. Samuel had told David he found it in his yard. He quickly ruled out some special candy that was left from a broken piñata. He thought about a leprechaun and a pot of gold, but decided that Samuel could not keep a leprechaun hidden in his garage. When he finally fell sleep, David was no closer to discovering the secret than he had been right after he talked to Samuel.

David was anxious for Gabriella's birthday so he could find out what Samuel was hiding in the garage. Finally the day came. As soon as David and his family arrived at Samuel's house, Samuel tugged on David's arm to follow him. The two of them walked quickly through the back hall and entered the garage without being noticed.

Samuel turned on the light and went directly to the hiding place. He removed the map, opened it and showed the map to David. He asked David, "Can you read the words on the paper?"

David had a sinking feeling. He hadn't been interested in learning how to read. He knew the letters, but couldn't read the words. Now he knew what his mom meant when she told him someday soon he would be upset with himself because he hadn't made any effort to learn how to read.

David looked at the map and tried to decipher some of the words, but he was unsuccessful. He was embarrassed. Finally he admitted to Samuel, "I can't read this. I don't know what it says."

As the two boys stared at the map, they tried to interpret it. They saw a drawing of a tree and a hill on the map. "Doesn't that look like the tree and hill in our backyard? And look at the small house. That could be our shed," whispered Samuel.

"Let's go find out," David replied. "I think we can do this. We don't need to read the words."

It was getting dark as the two boys began their adventure. They snuck around the corner of the garage and checked the backyard. No one was out there. After waiting a few minutes to make they were alone, they quietly moved from the garage to the yard. As they walked farther from the house, the light from the kitchen window began to fade.

"We need more light," said Samuel. "Wait here and I'll get a flash light."

"I think I'll go with you," responded David. "I don't want to be out here by myself in the dark."

Both boys ran back to the garage to get a flashlight. They crowded together, following the flashlight beam as they slowly moved toward the big tree.

When they got on the other side of the tree, Samuel put the map on the ground. As they were trying to pick out different items on the map, they heard a loud screech from somewhere high in the trees. The boys froze and stared wide-eyed at each other.

"Do you have an owl in your yard?" David asked.

"I don't think so," answered Samuel.

When the noise stopped, they waited for a few minutes before they resumed their quest. While David held the flashlight, Samuel tried to decipher the markings on the map.

"See that small building near the bottom of the map? There's an X behind it. I bet the treasure is behind the shed."

Each boy summoned the courage to start the trek. They moved in slow motion toward the shed. David was in front with the flashlight and Samuel close behind with the map. When the boys were about halfway to the shed, they heard another screech. This one was louder and closer than the last one. David flashed the light up into the trees. Two luminous eyes stared back at them. The creature lurched forward.

David and Samuel turned and dashed back toward safety. When they reached the house they ran inside and quickly slammed the door. Both boys were gasping and shaking.

After they calmed down, Samuel spoke first. "How 'bout we show the map to my dad and ask him join the treasure hunt?"

David nodded in agreement. They found Samuel's dad in the kitchen. Samuel showed him the map while David tried to explain what had happened.

Instead of being surprised, he just laughed. "Where did you boys find this map?"

Samuel said, "I found it in a pile of leaves in the backyard. We tried to read it, but we couldn't."

His dad chuckled again. "I must've left it there. This was one of the clues I had prepared earlier this month for the annual scavenger hunt for your older cousins. When the hunt didn't happen, I thought I picked up all the clues. I guess I forgot one."

Then he added, "If both of you learn to read by next year, maybe you could be part of the scavenger hunt."

Samuel and David looked at one another and began to laugh. They had an adventure but would have to wait for another opportunity to find a hidden treasure.

Erin and Maddie's Story

To the outside world Erin and Maddie are indistinguishable. The girls are classic identical twins. They look alike, talk alike, often think and act alike. They enjoy each other's company, feed off one another's energy and spend a lot of time together laughing and talking. They are complementary parts to the whole.

To each other, though, they are distinct. Both love having a sister the same age, but each wants to be her own person. Because of this, the twins decided they wanted to be in different classrooms when starting school. The girls had the support of their parents, and the school complied with their wishes.

The separation didn't prevent the girls from getting together each day after school. During one afternoon gab and play session they began talking about the story that Grandpa was going to write about them at Christmas. They knew they would be the main characters, but they didn't have any clues about its content.

After a few minutes, Erin came up with an idea. "Why don't we write our own story and read it to Grandpa? He'll be surprised."

Maddie wasn't convinced this was a good idea, but Erin persisted. "We could each think of a story and get Abby to write them down."

Maddie began to warm up to the idea. The more they chatted, the more excited they became. They talked about different ideas for the story. Maddie came up with the idea of writing a story about a pretend adventure with someone else in the family. Erin squealed with delight over this possibility.

Before Erin and Maddie could get started with their stories, they had to convince their sister, Abby, to assist with the project. Even though both girls could read well, they were not confident they could write their own stories.

Erin and Maddie approached Abby about their proposal. After listening and sensing their excitement, she agreed to help. However, in teacher-like fashion, Abby had one condition. "Each of you has to come up with a complete story before I start writing it down."

Erin and Maddie agreed and began working on their stories. Within a week they had finished products for Abby to transcribe.

Erin's Story

Erin wanted to go to the zoo with her siblings and cousins during their visit to Grandma and Grandpa's house at Christmas time. Grandma had an extended family pass and everyone liked visiting the zoo. They normally went during warmer weather. This time would be different. It was a chance to see the animals in winter.

After the presents had been opened at their Christmas celebration, Erin began executing her plan. She had already talked to Maddie and Abby about her approach. Each of them had assigned tasks to complete. Abby was to talk to the cousins her age and convince them that a winter zoo trip would be fun. Erin knew Abby would handle the task flawlessly.

Maddie was responsible for persuading their cousins Riley, Samuel and David to join the fun. Erin knew that Maddie had an easy job since those boys loved going to the zoo. If the boys were in favor, Molly, Gabriella and Sophia would easily follow.

Erin saved the most difficult tasks for herself. She had to convince her older brothers, Alex and Sean, to support her plan and get them talk it up with their cousins Christopher, Andrew, Matthew and Thad. Then Erin had to talk to her oldest sister, Meghan, and get her to convince Frances and DJ to be a part of the group. Erin needed the older girls and boys to convince the parents this was a good idea.

The plan went off almost without a hitch. The only hiccup was the older boys. At first Alex and Sean resisted and didn't want to go. But Erin said, "You owe me for all your baseball games I've had to attend."

They reluctantly agreed. "Okay. We'll convince the other guys to go."

Meghan was excited about the trip, and Frances and DJ quickly lent their support. The older girls used their charm to persuade the parents to join the party. They said, "It'll give Grandma and Grandpa a few hours of quiet when everyone is at the zoo." To their surprise, Grandma and Grandpa decided to go with the group.

Since Aunt T was not a cold weather person, she said, "I'll stay with the baby."

With everyone dressed in their winter jackets, hats, gloves or mittens, and boots, five fully stuffed vans arrived at the zoo. Even the weather was complying. It was snowing, but the temperature was in the low 30s. The group decided they would stay for a few hours and see as much as they could during that time. They split up into smaller groups and agreed to meet at the Family Farm at five o'clock.

As Erin's group was walking towards the elephant area, she was feeling very good about the day. She was at the zoo, and everyone seemed to be having fun. They had been to Monkey Island and the ape house, and had seen the large cats and the new baby hippo.

A loud trumpet sound interrupted her thoughts. When Erin looked for the source of the noise, she saw a baby elephant stuck in a crevasse. The young elephant was struggling to get out but kept slipping in the snow. A much larger elephant, which Erin assumed to be the mother, was standing on the ledge above and bellowing. She kept reaching down with her trunk, but the baby elephant would not grab it because it kept slipping. Watching this frustrating scene play out in front of her, Erin had an idea. She quickly conferred with Maddie and both decided plan might work.

Erin told everyone in her group to make a snowball and throw it at the baby elephant. The baby might be so afraid of being hit with the snow balls that it would reach for its mother's trunk to escape. There was only one problem. No one in Erin's group could throw a snow ball as far as the baby elephant.

Erin knew the older boys could reach the elephant with the snowballs. After a quick phone call, the boys arrived within minutes. They welcomed the challenge. Their arms were already loose because they had been throwing snow balls at the girls and each other for much of the afternoon. After a few warm-up throws they began to reach the target. When three snow balls hit the baby elephant at once, it panicked and jumped upward to reach the mother's trunk. The larger elephant grabbed tightly and pulled her baby out of the trough. After checking to make sure her baby was not hurt, she looked at the group and bellowed her thanks. Then the two moved off to a safer haven.

Everyone congratulated Erin on her quick thinking. Alex complimented her. "This was the most fun I've had in a long time."

When everyone got together at five o'clock, the elephant story was the topic of conversation.

Everyone was still buzzing about the zoo when they arrived back to Grandma's house. To their surprise, Aunt T had made hot chocolate for everyone. When all had been served, Christopher raised his cup and offered a toast to Erin.

"To Erin for a great afternoon at the zoo and for her quick thinking that rescued the baby elephant."

Everyone joined in a chorus of cheers and clicked their cups together.

Maddie's Story

Maddie's first day as a teacher was about to begin. She was excited and nervous. Maddie had dreamed of being a teacher ever since she and Erin attended her sister Abby's "after-school school." As a result of Abby's training, both girls were advanced beyond the other students in their grade. Each of them could read before they started school; each could write grammatically correct paragraphs before they started writing complete sentences in class. Maddie realized the reason she and her sister excelled was because Abby took the time to work with them. Maddie wanted to do the same for other children. She wanted to be that person who made the difference.

There was one peculiar circumstance about her new class. When reviewing her class list, Maddie noticed that her parents' names were included on the roster. She wasn't sure how it happened, but her mom and dad were in her third grade class. Now she was faced with the task of teaching her parents.

When the new third graders walked through the door, Maddie observed them carefully. Some looked excited while others appeared apprehensive. A few looked like they wanted to be anywhere but in school. The latter two groups would be her challenge.

As she watched, Maddie pictured herself in a similar situation not too many years ago. She had a great time in grade school and now she was trying to create the same experience for other children. Her dream was about to become a reality.

After all the other students were in their seats, her mom and dad walked into the classroom. Her mom gave a quick wave and both of them sat in the back of the room.

As soon as the bell rang, Maddie carefully wrote her name on the board and turned to address the class for the first time. She began her well-rehearsed introduction.

"Welcome to the third grade. I am Miss Noel and I'll be your teacher. I hope this year will be a great experience for you. We'll work hard but we'll also have fun. Learning is exciting.

"It's a lifelong journey. As your teacher I'll help you grow in knowledge and appreciation for learning. But I can't do it alone. Each of you will have to make the effort for all of us to be successful."

Maddie seemed to have their attention. She sensed her parents' presence in the back of the room, but tried not to pay attention to them.

"How many of you play a musical instrument?"

A few hands went up. Maddie asked one of the boys who had raised his hand, "What instrument do you play?"

"Piano," he responded.

"How long have you been playing piano?"

"About a year."

"How long are you supposed to practice each day?"

"My piano teacher wants me to practice a half-hour each day."

"If you don't practice, how well will you able to play your lesson?"

"Not so good. My teacher can always tell when I don't practice."

Maddie nodded to the boy and continued with her lecture. "Learning math or spelling or any other subject is the same thing. If you pay attention in class and do your assignments at home, you'll get better. But if you don't work, you won't improve."

Maddie began to feel more comfortable but was still concerned about her parents being in the classroom. They hadn't made a sound, but it was a problem for her. A few of the students turned to get a peek at the two adults sitting in the back.

She spent some time discussing classroom behavior. Maddie knew that she had been talking too long so she decided to have some student interaction. She asked each student to stand, tell their first and last name, if they had any pets and their favorite subject in school. She knew most of the boys would say either gym or recess, but she wanted to learn their names and find out a little more about each of them. She bypassed her parents and felt very bad for omitting them.

By lunchtime Maddie was frustrated. Even though her parents had not said a word, she did not feel in charge. She decided she had to ask them not to continue in her class. With her mind made up, Maddie approached her parents, who were sitting by themselves at a lunch table. She asked if she could talk to them privately. As they followed her back to the classroom, Maddie decided how she would explain her dilemma.

Before she could start the conversation, her mom said,

"Maddie, we're so happy to have the chance to be in a class that our daughter is teaching. How many other parents have had this opportunity? We're so proud of you."

Maddie gulped, but knew she had to persevere.

"Mom and Dad, you know I love you both and would never do anything to hurt you. But I have to talk to you about this classroom arrangement. Do you remember when Erin and I started school? We decided that we wanted to be in different classes so we could each be our own person. Now I have a similar problem. I can't be myself with you sitting there. Since I'm the teacher, I have to ask both of you not to continue in my class. It isn't fair to the other students."

When she finished, Maddie felt terrible. Her mom and dad didn't say a word. They nodded, gave Maddie a hug and walked toward the door. Before they reached the door, they turned and smiled. Her dad couldn't hold back any longer.

"Maddie, we weren't going to stay in your class. We asked the principal if we could observe your first morning. We're not sure how our names got on the class roster. Even though we caused you some discomfort, we're happy we were able to share the first day of your dream."

With that comment both of them waved, closed the door and walked into the hall.

The afternoon was more comfortable for Maddie. When the bell rang at the end of the day, Maddie could not believe how quickly the day had passed. As her students were leaving, one smiling girl stopped.

"Miss Noel, I had a great first day and look forward to the rest of the year."

Maddie returned her smile.

As she left the school building later that afternoon, Maddie couldn't wait to call Erin and Abby and tell them about her first day.

Molly's Story

Molly came downstairs while the other kids were getting ready for school. Instead of turning on television, which she normally did in the morning, Molly sat at the table while Noel, Lexi and Riley finished their breakfast. She announced to everyone that she had a very strange dream last night. Without any prompting, she started telling them her dream.

"Mom, do you remember when Grandpa called the five Dora candles on my birthday cake five little Mollys? Last night I had a dream about five Mollys. I was standing in front of the mirror in our bathroom and saw five Mollys staring back at me. The mirror was full of Mollys, but each one was dressed differently. As I looked at them, each Molly introduced herself. The first Molly said she was Learning Molly, and had a backpack full of books. The next one said she was Dancing Molly; she wore a bright red tutu and did a pirouette in the mirror. The third one said she was Fun Molly; she wore a funny hat and gave me a great big smile. The fourth one said she was Shy Molly and then hid behind one of the others. The last one said she was Mischievous Molly and winked at me. I could see five girls, but they all looked like me.

"Before I knew it Mischievous Molly grabbed my hand and pulled me into the mirror. Then all of them started running down a road. I followed along because I didn't know what else to do. I asked where we were going, but no one else seemed to care. Fun Molly produced a jump rope from somewhere and started skipping rope as we ran. After a while we slowed down and began to walk. Finally we stopped near a huge tree beside a large field. I was getting more worried about where we were, but I was the only one. None of the other girls seemed to care.

"Dancing Molly decided she was going to practice her ballet and began gracefully twirling and swirling in the field. Learning Molly sat at the base of the tree, pulled a book from her backpack and began to read. Mischievous Molly climbed the tree and began tossing twigs at the rest of us. Fun Molly tried to organize a game of tag. When I again asked about where we were, Fun Molly said I worried too much. She decided to call me Worry Molly."

"Molly, I'm sorry but you'll have to stop your story right there," said Mom. "These kids need to leave for school immediately or they'll be late."

Riley began to protest. "I want to hear more about Molly's dream."

One stern look from his mother quickly changed his mind. He grabbed his jacket and backpack and headed for the door.

Mom began ushering Noel and Lexi toward the door as the school bus braked in front of their driveway.

Molly poured herself a bowl of dry cereal and turned on the television, but she couldn't get the dream out of her mind.

All morning Molly wanted to tell someone about her dream. Nothing else seemed to interest her. After she tried watching television, she tried reading a book. Finally she asked her mom if she could call Grandma.

When Grandma answered the phone, she asked Molly, "Are you smiling? Normally I can tell from your voice when you are smiling. This morning it doesn't sound like you have a smile on your face."

Molly tried to explain to Grandma that she had this special dream last night about five Mollys and she couldn't finish telling anyone about it.

"Molly, unfortunately I'm running late and have to leave for Hospice soon. I can't talk right now. I'll call you later to hear about your dream."

Molly said good-bye and hung up the phone dejectedly.

The rest of the day dragged. Finally the kids came home from school. Her mom quickly served an after-school snack. Then Molly continued telling them about her dream.

"The group was still sitting around the big tree when an ugly old man approached us. He had long, wispy gray hair, a scraggly beard and a strange-looking hat on his head. He wore tattered clothes and carried a walking stick.

"We huddled together. He grunted something that none of us heard. Then he shouted, 'Why are you trespassing on my property?'

"Learning Molly spoke up. 'We didn't know that this was private property. We didn't mean any harm. If you would give us directions on how to get off your property, we'll gladly leave.'

"He sneered at that response. 'I'll do no such thing. Since you're on my property, I'll decide what to do with all of you.'

"We squirmed and looked anxiously at each other. After long, agonizing minutes during which he paced back and forth in front of us, he finally spoke. 'I will give you directions back home if you can correctly answer three questions. However, if you do not answer the questions correctly, you will remain here and be my servants. I have plenty of work for you to do.'

"Mischievous Molly spoke up this time. 'What'll happen if we choose not to play your silly game?'

"The old man glared at her. Mischievous Molly almost started crying.

"Finally he spoke. 'Missy, I don't think you have much choice. If you don't answer the question, I'll consider that a wrong answer and you'll lose the bargain. Like I said, I have a lot of work that will keep all of you busy for a long, long time.'

"As he spoke, a large, mangy dog suddenly appeared from nowhere and began circling our group. The animal sent a collective shudder through us.

"'In case any of you might be thinking of trying to run, that ugly mutt would like nothing better than to run you down and drag you back to me.'

"The old man leaned on his walking stick and pondered his next comment. We were afraid to look directly at his foul features.

Mischievous Molly hid her face with her hands. Shy Molly slid behind Dancing Molly.

"'I enjoy riddles,' the old man finally said. 'So the three questions I have for you will be riddles. Each one will be a little harder than the last one. You'll have a few minutes to decide on the answer. If you answer correctly, you will advance to the next question. If you're wrong or if you fail to answer, I will put all of you to work. Here is the first question. There was a competition where the contestants had to hold something the longest. The winner was a person with no hands or feet. How is that possible?'

"'I think I know the answer,' whispered Learning Molly. 'Since the winner had no hands or feet, she must have held her breath the longest.'

"'I think you're right,' said Fun Molly. 'Go ahead and give that crabby old man your answer.'

"We all nodded our assent, and Learning Molly said out loud, 'We have the answer. The winning contestant held her breath the longest.'

"The stranger smiled cynically. 'That was the easy one. Now they'll get harder. Here is the next question. There were six little girls walking to school. They were sharing one umbrella. When they arrived at school, none of them was wet. How is this possible?'

"We stared at each other. Finally Dancing Molly said, 'We have to stop worrying about what might happen and try to answer the question. Picture all of us walking to school with only one umbrella. How could we not get wet?'

"Shy Molly said, 'That umbrella would have to be really big so we could all fit under it. Still, someone would get wet from the rain because we couldn't all stay covered the whole way to school.'

"'That's it!' yelled Dancing Molly. 'You said someone would have to get wet from the rain because the umbrella could not possibly stay over everyone. The only way we could arrive at school without getting wet is if it wasn't raining.'

"The rest of us gave our thumbs up. 'Sir,' Dancing Molly said politely, 'we think the answer to that question is that it was not raining.'

"The old man winced and grudgingly admitted she was correct. 'Hopefully you'll not be successful with your next response. Here's the final question. There are two of these in every room and one of them in every corner. What is it?' He smirked.

"We huddled once more and started spouting possible answers. None of them made any sense. Shy Molly started drawing in the dirt with one of the twigs that Mischievous Molly had tossed at them earlier. She tried to make a picture of a room and next to it a picture of a corner. She was hoping the pictures would help her solve the riddle.

"When Fun Molly looked at the two drawings, she said, 'I don't know which one is the room and which one is the corner.'

"Frustrated, Shy Molly started to write the words below each picture. She stopped after writing the first word. 'Learning Molly, how do you spell corner?'

"As Learning Molly started to spell the word, Shy Molly shrieked, 'I know the answer! It is the letter O.'

"As she started to explain the word room has two Os and the word corner has one O, there was a bright flash and the old man and his mangy dog were gone.

"Then I woke up."

"Wow, that was quite a dream!" her mom exclaimed.

After pausing to think how to phrase her question, her mother asked Molly, "Do you realize all those Mollys were different versions of you?"

Molly gave her mother a big smile. "I guess I'm a pretty complicated character."

Gabriella's Story

Gabriella could not wait to move into her new house. During the days before the move, she packed games and stuffed animals in boxes so that they would be easy to move. With her sister's help, they carefully hung all their play dresses on hangers so they would have them in their new home. Gabriella envisioned playing princess in their spacious upstairs hallway overlooking the family room. It seemed like a perfect setting for a princess to look out over her domain.

After the move Gabriella had fun exploring her new home. She and Sophia had a new bedroom, the girlie room, to decorate and make their own. All the stuffed animals they had packed needed a new place to stay.

Of all the places she had explored at her new house, she liked being in her yard the best. She enjoyed working with her dad in their new yard, playing on the swing set and in the sandbox, and creating secret trails through the tall grass and trees. Even the cold weather did not discourage her from enjoying their spacious yard. She would beg Sophia to stay outside with her in the cold, but Sophia would abandon her and return to the warmth of the house.

One morning when it was especially cold, Gabriella decided she would not even try talking Sophia into going outside. Instead she asked Sophia to play dress up. They put on their special princess dresses and went into their brother Samuel's bedroom to play. They were pretending they were dancing under the stars when Gabriella saw something in the back of Samuel's closet she had not noticed previously. She crawled in to get a closer look.

In the back of the closet was a small door. It was closed and sealed, but it was definitely a door. She ran her hand around the edge and then pushed it to see if it would open. It didn't budge. Gabriella's imagination began to work overtime. *What could possibly be on the other side of the door?*

When Sophia called her to come back and play, Gabriella decided to wait until Samuel came home from school before pursuing this discovery.

As soon as Samuel dropped his backpack in the hall, Gabriella was at his side, urging him to come upstairs. Samuel first went into the kitchen to say hi to their mom and talk about his day at school. Gabriella waited impatiently until he finished and pleaded with him to go upstairs with her. "Please come with me. I want to show you something."

Finally he agreed and followed her upstairs. She went directly to his closet and pointed at the back wall.

"Have you seen that door?"

"I've seen it, but I didn't think much about it."

"Try to open it so we can see what's on the other side."

Samuel pushed the door with his hands. It didn't budge. He tried using his shoulder, but there was no movement. Then he saw the nails at the edge of the door and realized that he could not open it. He showed Gabriella the nails.

"There's no way we can open this door."

"Samuel, what if there's a secret passageway on the other side of that door? What if someone hid something behind the door? We have to find a way to get that door opened and find out what's behind it."

"Gabriella, it's nailed shut. We can't open it."

He started to leave the closet. Gabriella knew she had to act quickly.

"Find a flashlight and I'll get Sophia. We'll meet back in the closet and pretend to go through the door."

Samuel shrugged and decided to go along with her fantasy.

When the three of them returned to the closet, they slid the door closed and Samuel turned on the flashlight. Sophia was confused about what was going on but was content to be included in the group.

Gabriella began, "Let's hold hands, close our eyes, count to ten and pretend we're on the other side of the little door."

When they finished counting and opened their eyes, the three of them were in a different place. Still sitting and holding hands, they looked around and tried to figure out where they were. Not recognizing anything, they stood up and started walking down a path in front of them. The path seemed to be cut out of overgrown wilderness. After a short time they encountered an older boy who looked like he was a teenager.

He introduced himself and then did a strange thing. He removed his hat, bowed slightly and said, "At your service, Princess."

Gabriella began to introduce herself, Samuel and Sophia.

"No need to introduce yourself, Princess," said the boy. "I know who you are. I saw you and wondered why you were so far from your home. I decided to follow along to see if you needed help."

Before Gabriella could respond, she glanced down and saw that she and Sophia were still wearing their princess dresses from earlier in the day. This boy was obviously confused by their appearance and mistook her for someone else. Instead of correcting him, Gabriella decided to play along.

"Thank you for your kindness," she said.

Gabriella quickly signaled to Samuel and Sophia not to say anything. The four started walking in silence and soon came to an impressive-looking estate. It consisted of several buildings surrounded by a large iron fence. When they approached the gate, it swung open.

As they paused in front of the entrance, the older boy said, "Princess, I'm happy to have helped you return home. Now, with your permission, I'll be on my way."

Not knowing what to do, Gabriella nodded and the boy left them.

The three of them stood at the gate, unsure of what to do next.

Samuel spoke up. "I don't know what's going on, but I think we should turn back."

"Let's see what happens," countered Gabriella.

While they were still debating, a woman came out of one of the buildings and waved to them. She appeared to be summoning them to that building. Gabriella grabbed Sophia's hand and began walking toward the building. Samuel didn't want to leave his sisters alone, so he reluctantly followed.

As they entered the building they saw several children running around and playing. A few waved to them. They were in a large room with several small tables like their play table at home. As they stood watching, the woman who had waved walked up to them.

"I'm glad you're back, Princess. I was afraid that we would have to start the tea party without you."

Gabriella's eyes widened and she looked quizzically at Samuel. He returned her gaze with a shrug. *This is the second person that had called me Princess.*

While they were trying to figure out what was happening, the woman clapped her hands. "Everyone take your seats because the tea party is about to begin."

Gabriella looked for a table for the three of them. Even though she was the one who wanted to proceed, she didn't want to be separated from her brother and sister. While she was looking, the woman motioned them to a table in the middle of the room. It was different from the other tables because it had a tablecloth and pillows on the chairs.

"Here is your table, Princess. The cookies and hot chocolate will be brought out immediately."

As soon as Gabriella sat down, a young woman brought out a tray with cups and saucers, a pitcher of hot chocolate and a plate of cookies. She placed a cup and saucer in front of Gabriella and immediately poured her hot chocolate. Then she offered the cookies for Gabriella's selection. Samuel looked around and noticed that no one else in the room was being served. Everyone was watching Gabriella. After she had finished serving Gabriella, the young woman served Samuel and Sophia.

The woman spoke to the other children. "Now the Princess is served, you may go to the serving table for your hot chocolate and cookies."

Samuel looked across the table and whispered to Gabriella. "We should leave."

Gabriella shook her head. "It's fun being treated like a princess."

Samuel responded, "It may not be much fun if someone discovers you're not a real princess."

When all of the children returned to their tables with hot chocolate and cookies, a clown rode through the doorway on a unicycle. He was juggling three large balls.

"Would anyone like balloon animal?"

The children yelled enthusiastically.

The clown jumped off the unicycle and walked directly to Gabriella. He took off his small hat and bowed with a flourish.

"Do you have a color preference, Princess?" he asked.

"Pink," answered Gabriella.

He grabbed a pink balloon from his pocket, waved it for all to see and blew it up. He twisted the balloon several times and made a dog. When he finished, he knelt on one knee and presented the balloon character to Gabriella. Then he stood up, remounted the unicycle and pedaled to the other side of the room. He began making several balloon characters and stacking them on a table.

This time Samuel was insistent.

"Princess or no princess, we're leaving."

Not giving Gabriella a chance to refuse, he grabbed Gabriella and Sophia by the hand and started walking to the door. All the activity in the room stopped. Everyone watched as the three hurried from the room.

As Samuel pushed opened the door, he heard someone shout, "Wait!"

Without a backward glance, he grabbed Gabriella and Sophia and started to run. Turning around, he saw some people starting to chase them. After a short distance, he stopped and looked directly into his sisters' eyes.

"Hold hands, close your eyes, count to ten and wish yourself back to my closet."

At ten they opened their eyes and found themselves sitting in the dark closet. Before they could talk about what had just happened, there was a knock on the door.

"Gabriella, Samuel, Sophia, are you in there? I've been looking all over the house for you. We're ready to eat. Come downstairs, wash your hands and get ready for dinner."

As they tumbled out of the closet, Gabriella told Samuel and Sophia she wanted to tell their story at dinner. The other two agreed.

After she finished, her dad looked at them and said, "Kids, that was a wild adventure. Maybe I should have a closer look in that closet. Also, remember this lesson. As you grow older you'll find that it's more fun being yourself than pretending to be someone else. Besides, it's a lot safer."

Sophia's Story

Despite her diminutive size, Sophia's charisma makes her the center of any group or activity in which she participates. When she smiles, she brightens a room. Her sad face leaves nothing to the imagination.

When playing outside at home, Sophia usually gets her way. If she wants to play soccer, the group plays soccer. Occasionally Samuel exercises his oldest-child-in-the-family privilege and insists on playing something other than what Sophia wants. Then she reluctantly concedes but employs the sad face as necessary.

In school, she takes over in the classroom or at recess. She is the one who picks the activities and the teams. Even the boys go along with her decisions.

Sophia is also a good student, perhaps too good. She is normally the first one finished with her work. That gives her time to do other things. Sometimes she helps her classmates complete their assignments. Mrs. Gross appreciates her generosity, but prefers these students do their own work. Sometimes she just sits back and daydreams.

Her daydream of choice is about gymnastics. Since she and Gabriella started gymnastics several months ago, Sophia has been passionate about the sport. She does two-handed and one-handed cartwheels at the hint of an audience.

One morning after completing her class work she just sat back in her chair and imagined what it would be like to participate in gymnastics in the Olympics. She and Gabby Douglas as teammates — what a pair!

Before gymnastics class the following week her teacher told the group, "For the next several weeks we'll be focusing on improving the routines we've been learning. During the last part of each class all of you will perform on each apparatus. I'll grade everyone's performance and post the scores and comments on the side board. Your goal should be to reduce your deficiencies and increase your scores from week to week. If everyone progresses like I think they should, the final class will be a full gymnastics program."

The competitive juices in Sophia began to flow. Even though the teacher said this was not a contest among the students, Sophia decided she wanted to be the best in each event.

When she got home from gymnastics that evening, she told her dad, "I'd like to have the highest score in each event. If we set up a balance beam, bars, a springboard and a mat in the basement, then Gabriella and I could practice every night."

Not wanting to dampen her enthusiasm, her father agreed to help out. "I can build a beam and find a mat somewhere. But, I don't think we'll be able to put bars and a spring board in the basement."

When he finished the beam and located a mat on Craigslist, their basement began to look like a gym.

Sophia created a practice schedule so she could spend a certain amount of time on each exercise. If she was going to be the best, she knew she had to work for it. Both Laura and Lacy, two older girls in the class, had taken gymnastics longer than Sophia and were more advanced in the various events.

After eight weeks of scoring, Sophia had the highest marks in the class on balance beam. She was second on floor exercise and third on the bars and vaulting.

Because of the overall improvement in the group, the teacher kept her promise. The last class was to be an all-around competition. The students would participate in each event and receive a score for that event. After the four events, the numbers would be added together for a total score for the all-around. To make it more authentic, three outside people from the Carroll University gymnastic club would be judging the performances.

Before the start of the meet, the judges met with all the participants. "Since all of you will be performing the same routines, we will be using a modified version of the International Gymnastics Federation scoring system. You will be graded on the execution, precision and style of your movements. Points will be deducted for falls and failure to complete the routine within the time limit."

The first event was the balance beam. Each participant had to perform five compulsory moves on the beam in ninety seconds. If the student fell off, she had to get back on the beam and complete the routine in the allotted time.

Sophia was the third in line. She watched intently as the first two participants struggled through their routines. The first girl fell off the beam and didn't finish. The next stumbled badly and had to grab the beam with both hands to prevent a fall. Then she hurried through the rest of the routine and performed badly. Both scores were low.

When it was her turn, Sophia mounted the beam with confidence. After all, she had the highest grade in the class on this apparatus. Sophia completed the required two dance elements and was making a turn on one foot when she lost her balance and slipped off the beam. Her face turned as red as her tights as both feet touched the floor. She regained her composure, remounted and finished her routine. Her dismount was flawless.

The judges consulted and reached a consensus. Despite the deduction for a fall, Sophia's score was well above the two previous competitors. But there were five other students who still had to perform on the beam.

Laura and Lacy performed as expected and were first and second in scoring after the first event. Sophia was a distant third.

The next event was the bars. Sophia knew that this was not her best event, but her scores had jumped almost a full point in the last two weeks. The rotation for this event was reversed and Sophia was third from the end. She watched her two primary competitors perform clean routines. As she chalked her hands, she knew that she needed a big score to have a chance.

She grasped the bar and began her first move. Ninety seconds later she did a final twirl and stuck her dismount with only a slight movement of her feet. She flung out her arms and smiled broadly.

After the judges scored her performance, Sophia moved into a second place tie with Lacy. Laura was still in first, but her lead shrank.

The springboard was the most difficult event for all the students. They had to run down the lane, hit the board, spring into the air, do a front flip and land with both feet planted firmly on the mat. Spotters stood on both sides of the mat to catch errant efforts.

No one performed well on the springboard, and all the scores were low. The leader board didn't change.

Floor exercise was the final event. This was the activity that she and Gabriella had practiced the most. Because Sophia was third from the end, she had to watch both Laura and Lacy perform before her. Gabriella followed the two of them. When Gabriella finished her routine, Sophia gave her a big hug.

Now it was Sophia's turn. She stood on the corner of the mat, took a deep breath and began her run. She started with two one-handed cartwheels and a flip. She moved through the required dance and tumbling routines and finished with two back flips. As she knelt on one knee with her arms raised, Sophia knew that she had performed well.

When the last girl finished her routine, the judges gathered with the teacher. After a brief discussion, they announced to the group, "We are awarding three 'best in class' ribbons. Laura, Lacy and Sophia, please come forward and receive your ribbons."

Sophia beamed as she walked to the judges. She shook their hands, received her ribbon and did a cartwheel in front of everyone.

After the ribbons were presented, one of the judges took the teacher aside. "That little girl in the red tights has a lot of talent. We also liked her spunk. Did you see her after she fell off the beam? Instead of being discouraged, she got back on the beam and finished strongly. That's rare for someone that young. We suggest she be pushed ahead and get individual coaching. She's that good."

The teacher relayed the judge's comments to Sophia's mom and dad. She told them she could recommend a few coaches in the area that would be happy to work with Sophia.

On the way home, Dad asked Sophia, "Would you be interested in moving ahead in gymnastics and train with a different coach? The judges suggested it to your teacher. They think you have a special talent. You'd be with a small group of select kids and receive in-depth instructions. It would be far more intense than your current class."

Sophia thought for a moment. "I guess it would be fun to move ahead, but then I wouldn't be with Gabriella. I think I'll just keep practicing in the basement."

Julia's Story

With her backpack slung over her shoulders, Julia hopped from one foot to the other. She was eager to get going. On normal school days she rode the bus with her older brother and sisters, but not today. Her class was going on a field trip and she was being picked up at a different time.

When the bus finally arrived, Julia noticed this was not the regular school bus. It was much smaller and had funny looking flaps hanging from the side.

The driver swung open the door. Julia jumped up the first step and then stopped. She didn't recognize the person driving the bus. This driver had a large mustache and a strange hat. He smiled at Julia and waved her in.

"Where's Dave, the bus driver?" Julia asked.

"He's not drivin' this special run. I'm Fred and I'll be your driver for today. Come on in and find a seat. Welcome to the group."

Julia carefully walked up the next step. When she saw some of her classmates already seated, she relaxed a little and looked for a seat. Charlie waved and Julia sat next to her.

As Julia slipped out of her backpack, Charlie whispered, "Aren't you excited? I can hardly wait for the magic show."

After picking up the last child, the driver steered the bus to an empty field. He stopped, stood up and turned around. "Boys and girls, you're about to experience the ride of your life. Fasten your seat belts. We'll be taking off shortly for Funderland, the magicians' paradise! For your safety please stay in your seat with your seat belt on while the bus is in flight. Also, make sure your backpacks are tucked under the seat in front of you."

Julia quickly turned to Charlie. "Did he just say we're going to fly?"

Before Charlie could answer, they heard a screech and saw a wing lift up from their side of the bus. They looked out the window across the aisle and another wing appeared. Still staring at the wings, they heard a roar from the engine and the bus started racing across the field. The entire bus rattled and vibrated. The wings began to flap.

"Hang on!" the driver shouted over the noise. "Here we go!"

The bus lifted off the ground and began to soar. It circled the field once and headed west.

The girls sat frozen to their seats. Someone from the back of the bus screamed, "I'm scared! I wanna get off!"

The driver tried to comfort the group. "Don't be frightened. I know it's noisy, but this bus is completely safe. Today's a great day for flying. If we had to drive the whole way, it would take more than an hour. This way we'll get there in twenty minutes. Remember, we're on an adventure!"

As the bus leveled and the engine quieted down, the chatter picked up. Julia loosened her grip on the seat in front of her. She tried to look out the window. Charlie pointed to a cluster of small animals on the ground.

"I think they're cows, but they look so small."

After leaning out of her seat and looking around the bus, Julia nudged closer to Charlie. "Are we really flying? Where's Mrs. Gross and the chaperones?"

As if he had been listening, the driver announced, "We're flying at an altitude of 1500 feet. Mrs. Gross said she would meet us at the park entrance. She didn't think there would be enough room for the adults."

Emma, sitting directly behind Julia, leaned forward and said, "Did Mrs. Gross say anything in class about a special bus or flying to Funderland?"

110

Right on cue, the driver responded. "This is an experimental vehicle. Your teacher wanted this whole day to be an adventure. Sit back and enjoy the ride."

The girls glanced at one another but didn't say another word.

One of the boys across the aisle said to his seat mate, "My stomach's not doin' so good. I feel sick."

Again the driver answered, "If you're feeling sick, lean forward and put your head between your knees. If you think you're going to throw up, please use the bag that's in the seat pocket in front of you."

The boy immediately lowered his head between his legs.

"This is gettin' creepy," Julia whispered to Charlie. "It's like the driver can hear everything we say."

"No whispering," said the driver. "It's not polite. I have an idea. Let's sing a song. Who knows a song that everybody can sing?"

As the bus choir finished the song, the driver announced, "Check your seat belts and make sure they're snug. We'll be landing in less than three minutes."

The bus touched down and bounced twice before it drove safely on the ground. When it slowed, the kids could see the entrance to Funderland out the right-side windows. The bus came to a stop directly in front of the park.

"We're here! Don't forget to take your personal belongings with you. Have a great day!"

The kids cheered, grabbed their stuff and began piling off the bus. As Julia walked down the steps, she glanced back and saw the driver pull out something long, black and silky from beneath his seat.

Julia stepped onto the pavement and saw Mrs. Gross and the other chaperones standing at the gate waiting for them.

"Mrs. Gross, how did you get here so fast?"

The teacher answered, "We took an early bus."

Before anyone could comment on their strange ride, Mrs. Gross gathered them together. "Line up quickly. Let's go through the gate and get stamped. I've already paid for the tickets. If we hurry, we can go on a few rides before lunch. The magic show begins at twelve thirty."

When the class went through the entrance, Mrs. Gross separated the kids into two groups. She headed one group and Emma's mom was in charge of the other.

As the children headed for the rides, Mrs. Gross yelled, "We'll meet in the picnic area in ninety minutes for lunch."

After the Bouncing Balls, the Rocket Roller Coaster, the Celestial Sky Walk and the Lumber Log Jam, Mrs. Gross sensed the kids might be ready for a break.

"There are some colorful benches over there. Let's rest for a few minutes."

Despite a few protests, the group gathered around the benches. As soon as the first bench was occupied, it started to moan, "Get off me! You're too heavy!" The kids jumped off and the bench cheered.

When the other children saw what happened, they scrambled to sit on the other benches. Each reacted differently. One began to shake and sing, "I'm All Shook Up." Another moved slowly in a circle and crooned, "Ring Around the Rosy." A third moved up and down and yelled, "Ride 'em cowboy!" When one bench started to yell, "Help, I'm being held captive by a mad magician!" the kids laughed out loud.

After the youngsters tired of the antics of the benches, they headed to the picnic area for lunch.

During lunch, Mrs. Gross explained the plan for the afternoon. "You're going to have an adventurous walk to the magic show. I won't spoil the surprises. Be careful and try to stay together. When you arrive at the theater, sit close to the front so you can see the magician."

When everyone finished lunch, they again lined up in two groups, one behind the other. The kids started marching as they headed to the Magic Theater.

Mrs. Gross held up her hand in front of the entrance. "Walk through single file. I'll meet you on the other side."

Julia waited her turn and opened the door to a dimly lit room. As she entered, red, white and blue lights flashed in every direction. Laughter bellowed from a speaker and a booming voice cautioned, "You are about to enter the magnificent magician's weird walkway. If you stay alert and nimble, you will be rewarded with a magic show on the other side. Keep your heads up and eyes ahead."

A door on the opposite side of the room slid open and Julia walked through it. In front of her was a huge open-ended barrel spinning in a clockwise direction. A large sign above flashed *Barrel of Fun*. There was no room on either side to walk around, so the only way to the other side was through the barrel. As she stood waiting, Julia watched her classmates try to negotiate the rolling drum. They bumbled, stumbled and tumbled. One even crawled to the other side.

When Julia stepped into the barrel, she began to wobble and almost fell. She caught herself and began to giggle. Struggling to maintain her balance, she picked up the pace and proceeded in a zigzag fashion to the other end.

Confidently she approached challenge number two. In front of her was a long walkway with slats moving back and forth. Holding on to the sides Julia navigated the sliding boards without much trouble.

The next obstacle, labeled *Up the Down Staircase*, looked like an escalator. To be successful the kids had to climb up the downward moving stairs. After two false starts, Julia grabbed the railing with both hands, followed Evert and scrambled up the fifteen steps. When she and Evert reached the top, they saw side-by-side slides across the platform. Each grabbed a burlap bag from a large bin and raced to the top of the slide.

They flopped the bags down next to each other and hopped on. When their bottoms hit the burlap, the slides began to quiver. Evert slipped and darted down the shaky surface. Julia pushed off to try and catch him. As the two raced toward the bottom, a large overhead roller of soapsuds began advancing towards them. They screamed as they swooped through the bubbles. Evert's feet touched a mat at the bottom ahead of Julia. Cheers rang out and sparkling confetti sprinkled from the ceiling.

Laughing, both children headed to the exit door. As they pushed it open, bright sunshine greeted them. Many of their classmates were already gathered around Mrs. Gross. As the rest of the class finished the challenge, the group buzzed about the strange path to the magic show.

Mrs. Gross raised her hand and everyone quieted down. "Congratulations. It looks like everyone survived the adventurous walk. Now let's head to the theater for the show. Form two lines and follow me."

Julia and Charlie held hands and skipped to the theater. Once inside, the class scrambled for the front-row seats. Julia and Charlie landed in the middle of the second row.

After a brief wait, the lights dimmed and a speaker blared, "Ladies and gentlemen, and children of all ages! For your entertainment, the Funderland Park is proud to present the one, the only, Fabulous Fred. His sleight of hand, art of illusion and extraordinary feats of magic will amaze you!"

The stage went dark. Then a single spotlight shone on stage. A figure in dark clothing hidden behind a cloak rose slowly. As he unfurled his cape and stepped forward, Evert yelled, "That's Fred, our bus driver. See, he has on the same goofy hat."

The magician stood in the center of the stage and took a deep bow. When the cheering slowed, he raised his hand and spoke. "Welcome to our show! I hope you enjoy the various feats of magic we have prepared for you. During the performance I will select volunteers from our audience to assist me. No prior magic experience is necessary. Okay, let's get started."

Walking closer to the audience, he asked, "How many of you like to play cards?"

Several hands shot up.

"Good! I do too." Instantly he raised his right hand and produced a deck of cards out of the air.

"Young man in the blue shirt sitting on the aisle in the third row, would you please come up and join me?"

Conner looked down to make sure he had on a blue shirt. Then he jumped out of his seat and ran up the steps to the stage.

The magician motioned the boy to come closer. "What's your name?"

"Conner."

"Okay, Conner. You're going to help me with some card tricks. First, I want you to examine this deck of cards. Does it look like an ordinary deck of cards?"

The magician handed the deck to the boy. Conner looked at the deck, fanned through the cards, turned them over and examined the other side. "It looks normal to me."

Fred clapped twice and a table popped up from nowhere. He took the cards, quickly shuffled them three times, and spread them out on the table. He turned, reached in his pocket and threw something on stage. A loud bang echoed throughout the theater. Another table appeared about ten feet away.

The crowd gasped.

"Before we continue, Conner, I want you to walk over to the other table and examine the box sitting on it. Hold it up to the audience so they can see in it. Then place it back on the table."

Conner did as instructed, picked up the box, looked inside and showed the audience there was nothing in it.

"Now, I'm going to turn my back. I want you to pick a card from the deck I spread out on this table, show it to the audience and return it to the deck. Then straighten the cards so I can't see which card you picked. After you're finished, yell the magic words, 'I hope this works!'"

Conner did what he was told. When Fred heard the magic phrase, he turned and stared at the cards. "Conner, I think you're on your way to becoming a magician."

He reached to his side and pulled a wand out of his waistband.

Facing the audience, Fred shouted. "I want everybody count to three. When I hear three, I'm going to tap the deck once with this wand. After I tap, the card Conner picked will fly from the deck to that empty box. Watch carefully."

At the sound of three, Fred tapped the deck and quickly turned his head to follow the flight of the card. "Did you see it?"

Some of the audience shook their heads. The rest just sat there.

"Conner, go over to the box and see what's in it."

Doing what he was told, Conner walked to the box. He paused.

"Go ahead, Conner. Show everyone what's in the box."

Conner reached into the box and lifted out a kitten.

The audience squealed with delight.

"Conner, there must be a mistake. Hand me the kitty and see if there's anything else in the box?"

After receiving the kitten, the magician handed it to someone off stage. Conner walked back to the table. He peered into the box and pulled out a book.

Fred groaned. "Oh no! I don't understand! I heard you say the magic phrase. I saw the card fly into the box. What's the name of the book?"

Conner looked at the front of the book. *"Magic Tricks Made Easy,"* he called out.

"That's easy for you to say."

The kids giggled at the magician's comment.

"Conner, I want you to look through the book and see if there's any clue in there to help us out."

As Conner opened the book, something fell to the stage. He bent down, picked it up and showed it to the audience.

"It's the card I picked out of the deck," he shouted.

The magician bowed and everyone clapped loudly.

With Conner's assistance, Fred amazed the audience with several more card tricks. Finally, he took the deck in his left hand and turned to his helper.

"Conner, I need you to be observant. This is a magic card deck. Without it I can't do any card tricks. It's important that I don't lose it. Watch closely and see where it goes."

After those instructions Fred wrapped his left hand around the deck and held it in front of Conner. He grabbed the wand with his other hand, waved it slowly over his closed fist and struck his knuckles firmly.

Fred immediately began shaking his left hand. "Ow! That hurt! I didn't mean to hit it so hard."

Suddenly he stopped. "Conner, where'd the deck go? Do you

see it? Look around. I have to have those cards!"

Both of them searched the stage. Fred even got down on his knees and pulled a large magnifying glass out of his back pocket. "Maybe this'll help!"

After another minute of searching, Fred looked at the audience with a smile on his face. "You don't suppose. Naw, it can't be! Well, maybe, it's worth a try. Conner, check the box."

Conner ran over to the table and pulled the deck of cards out of the box. The magician gestured to Conner and bowed. The kids screamed with delight.

"Conner, thanks for your help. You've been a great assistant."

Three more times Fred selected children to help him on stage as he continued to perform his skillful magic.

After completing a trick connecting several separate large rings into a chain, Fred tossed them aside. With his arms open wide, he spoke to the group. "You've been wonderful this afternoon. I hope you enjoyed the show as much as I enjoyed putting it on. I have time for one more magic trick. With someone's help, I will attempt to make objects float in the air. For this trick to work, I need a strong-minded assistant. Do I have any volunteers?"

Almost everyone's hand shot up. Fred raised his right hand over his eyes to block the glare of the lights as he searched the crowd.

"Pick me, pick me, pleeease pick me!" yelled the kids.

"How 'bout the brown-haired girl with the yellow top in the middle of the second row?"

Everyone looked at Julia. Stunned by her selection, Julia froze. Charlie had to pry Julia out of her seat and push her toward the stage. Julia stumbled as she climbed the steps.

Fred reached out his hand. "Welcome. What's your name, young lady?"

"Julia," she half-whispered.

"Julia, for this next bit of magic to work, I need you to concentrate on an object. Do you think you can do that?"

Julia gulped and nodded. "I think so."

"Okay. We'll start with something small. Julia, stand next to the box on the table over there and focus on the box. Picture the box in your mind. I'm going to give you a handful of magic pixie dust. The audience and I will count to three. When we reach three, I want you to toss the magic dust in the air above the box and yell, 'Fly like a pixie!'"

Fred positioned Julia near the table and handed her a small amount of glitter. The stage lights narrowed on the box.

"Now remember, Julia, concentrate on the box."

Fred turned to the audience and signaled by raising one finger.

Everyone responded, "One . . . , Two . . . , Three!"

On three, Julia threw the glitter in the air and yelled, "Fly like a pixie!"

The dust sparkled in the light as it fluttered down on the table. A low rumble began to resonate throughout the front of the theater. The table started to shake and lifted off the stage. It hovered about two feet above the ground. Colorful streamers and confetti began flowing from the box. Twinkle lights like fireflies flew out of the opening and danced in the air. Then, a loud bang echoed across the stage and the box flew about ten feet in the air. Red and blue smoke trailed the container.

"Wow! Julia, you really know how to concentrate!" shouted the magician.

Julia stood wide-eyed and watched in amazement. The audience shouted their approval.

At that point the stage went dark. A few kids screamed.

When the lights came back on, the stage was empty, except for Julia. She looked around to see what was going to happen next. Silence.

Finally a voice came over the speaker. "That's the end of our show. Fred had to exit quickly so he asked me to say good-bye for him. Thanks for attending. We hope you had fun. And remember, there's magic all around us. Take time to enjoy the marvels we experience every day!"

Not knowing what to do, the kids just sat there. A few started to clap and cheer and the rest quickly joined them. Julia wandered back to her seat.

After the noise died down, Mrs. Gross stood up to address the group.

"The bus is waiting outside. We'll all be returning to school together. There's no special bus back. I think you've had enough adventure for one day."

As Julia and the rest of the kids exited the theater and waited to get on the bus, Julia glanced back at the building. Peeking out from around the corner was Fred. Julia waved, but before she could say anything, he tipped his hat and disappeared.